A CHRIST   T FOR
THE LORD

SWEET REGENCY ROMANCE

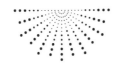

CHARLOTTE DARCY

JOIN MY NEWSLETTER

*P*uthall Abbey held many memories. Some good and some bad. For Madeline Crenshaw, her arrival at the place was tinged with sadness. The long corridors and plentiful rooms had held much happiness in the past, but not now. This time, she was there not as a guest, but as its inheritor. The sad passing of her Aunt Victoria had been the reason for her journey from London that day.

Victoria had been a strange woman. One who was wealthy in her own right and as such, she had ensured that her wealth passed to her niece. For now, Madeline could not think of such things. Her mind continued to drift, as it had throughout the journey.

In childhood, the abbey, with its seemingly endless gardens and unexplored rooms, had been a playground. Though an only child, she had found much delight in coming there to stay, and her Aunt Victoria had always been filled with a mischievous and adventurous spirit. Together they would have picnics in the drawing room on wet afternoons or roll down the banks out on the lawns when the weather was warm and sunny.

It was at Puthall that she had learned of the sad death of her father, killed whilst serving abroad. Only eight at the time, it had been hard to comprehend. They had wept together, as Agatha, her aunt's faithful housekeeper, had done her best to comfort them. In the time that followed, the abbey had become safety and comfort. It was a place that held a myriad of feelings, and with the sad passing of her beloved aunt it seemed to take on a different feel entirely.

"Is this it, ma'am?" the carriage driver asked as they came to the large and imposing gates, which were open, revealing a long tree-lined drive beyond.

"Yes, this is Puthall Abbey," she replied, pulling down the window and looking out.

The house was an imposing pile, though not as big as some of the other properties in the district. It was built of sandstone and had once been a Benedictine Convent, hence the name. The reformation had seen to all that, and the place had been gifted to an ancestor of the Crenshaw's who had set about turning it into the home it was today.

There were reminders of its ecclesiastical past everywhere, and the chapel of the convent now served as a fine dining room in which her aunt would often host parties. As they drove along the drive, Madeline pictured herself on numerous occasions when she would arrive with her parents... later only her mother, at the abbey. They would be invited for grand parties and balls, traveling up from London to stay with Aunt Victoria, who always indulged Madeline far more than her parents ever did.

Victoria had never married, and this had given her something of a youthful vitality and a spirit of adventure, which, even in her old age, she had never lost. Madeline felt an overwhelming sense of responsibility in inheriting the house and the estate. It had never occurred to her as a child that she would do so, but with no other living relative's,

Aunt Victoria had naturally left everything to her. The two had been close and corresponded regularly.

Madeline had last been at Puthall three months previously for a ball at the end of the summer season. It was one at which all manner of society figures had been in attendance. She had dutifully danced with any number of eligible young men, and her aunt had expressed her wish that Madeline soon find herself a young man with whom to settle down.

It was in this that the two disagreed, for Madeline was a spirited sort and not prone to court the affections of young men, however charming, they might seem. Her aunt had longed to see a wedding at Puthall Abbey. With the sad death of Madeline's mother just a year ago, the elderly spinster had taken it upon herself to assist her niece in finding a suitable match.

But Madeline, a spirited brunette and at only twenty-three, was not ready to settle down just yet. At least, that was what she had told her aunt, who had simply sighed and given her a disappointed look. It was this look which now haunted Madeline. She felt a sense of guilt that her dear Aunt Victoria, or

Vicky, as she used to call her, would never see her married.

The carriage drew up outside the house, and Madeline looked up at the imposing pile above. It was divided into three wings, with a central tower that must have once been the abbey belfry, but which was now turned over to bedrooms. The doors were open, and the servants had lined up to greet their new mistress, though all had known her since childhood.

Her aunt disliked change, and she had gathered about her a faithful group of servants headed by Mrs. Morrison, the housekeeper. Madeline knew her as Agatha, and before Milton, the footman, could step forward, she had thrown open the carriage door and jumped down. She never had been one to stand on ceremony.

"Agatha, how wonderful to see you, how wonderful to see you all," she said, turning to the servants and smiling.

"Yet under such sad circumstances, ma'am," Mrs. Morrison replied. There was a tear in her eye, and she embraced Madeline, tutting as she did so. "Look at me. I am all a flutter of nerves. But we have been waiting for your arrival, ma'am, and we want everything to be just right for you."

"I am sure it will be perfect. I have so looked forward to arriving, but yes, these are sad circumstances. It will take some time for us all to adjust to the loss of my dear Aunt Vicky," Madeline replied, as the footmen began to unload her bags.

"You must be tired, ma'am. Come inside, and you shall have a nice cup of tea in the drawing room," Mrs. Morrison said, ushering her inside.

Madeline took a deep breath and crossed the threshold. Inside, the house smelt as it always did, faintly of lavender and beeswax polish, a familiar and comforting smell which took her back to her childhood. Everything was just as she remembered it, and she wondered why she had imagined it would now be different? It had been only a few months since last she set foot in Puthall Abbey on the day of her aunt's funeral, yet so much had changed. The house, however, had not.

As she walked through the hallway, with its large and imposing portraits of past Crenshaws, the clocks began to chime the hour of four. Her aunt had always been a stickler for time and ensured that every clock in the abbey was kept wound and accurate. It was as though her aunt was welcoming her to what was now her home. As she settled herself in the drawing room, she smiled and looked up at the portrait of Aunt Vicky hanging on the wall.

It showed her in the gardens at Puthall, no older than Madeline was herself. She was wearing a pretty pink gown and a white bonnet, her hand resting on the head of one of her numerous dogs. She was smiling, her head raised, as though in an expression of the independence she had maintained throughout her life. It had always struck Madeline as strange that her aunt so wished for her to find a man to marry when she herself had so resolutely refused to do so. There had never been any love interest for Aunt Victoria, and her mother had once said that no man could possibly take on such a task as taming the wayward spinster of Puthall.

Madeline smiled to herself. Perhaps she too would adopt that attitude and live by the independent means by which her aunt had now allowed her to do. She had no need for marriage and besides, out here in the countryside she would hardly be exposed to the sort of society she had enjoyed in London. Since her coming out at the age of eighteen, her life had been punctuated by balls, soirees, dinners, and dances. All were designed to showcase the myriad of young ladies who were seeking precisely the same as the next. A husband. Madeline found such things dull, and recently, she had stopped attending such events, preferring her own company instead and that of the books she so delighted in. Madeline was an avid reader, she was looking forward to exploring more of her aunt's library.

"There we are, ma'am. A nice cup of tea for you, you must be tired after your journey," Mrs. Morrison said, bustling in with a silver tea tray in hand.

"It has certainly been a day of mixed emotions, Agatha," Madeline replied.

"Well, you must take your time to settle in. It is very different being the mistress of a house than being a visitor. But do not worry, ma'am, we shall see you right," the kindly housekeeper replied.

"And I am very grateful for that," Madeline replied. "I fear there will be many things I do not know, nor understand about running a house such as Puthall.

The Abbey has long been like a second home to me, but now it must become my first home, and there is something quite daunting about that."

"You will find this house a pleasant place to live in. I have been here some thirty years now, and there is not much I do not know about the abbey," Mrs. Morrison said, crossing over to the window, but as she did so, she let out a cry and turned to Madeline in horror. "A man, ma'am, riding over Mr. Lawson's lawn."

"What?"

"He has only clipped it this afternoon; how rude, how brazen. He must be from the village." She banged on the window. "Shoo! Off with you."

Madeline got up and crossed to the window with interest. There, she could see the source of Mrs. Morrison's displeasure. A man was cantering across the lawns, seemingly oblivious to the damage he was doing to Mr. Lawson's hard kept pristine lawn. The gardener prided himself upon keeping the ground of the abbey immaculate, despite the now encroaching winter weather, and Madeline could well remember his chastisement when, as a child, she had thought it a kindness to pick roses for her aunt without asking.

"Of all the nerve," Mrs. Morrison continued, shaking her head. "I do not know what this world is coming to, ma'am. There was a time when folks showed respect to other's property."

"I shall speak with this man," Madeline said, resolved to do something, now that Puthall Abbey was her own.

She had no intention of allowing men from the village to ride roughshod across her lawns. Her aunt would never have stood for such things, and neither would she. Picking up her skirts, she marched to the doors of the drawing room. They led out onto the terrace from which the laws stretched down to the brook. It formed the natural boundary of the abbey's gardens. To the left was the large walled garden and orchard where Mr. Lawson grew vegetables and fruits for the kitchen, whilst to the right was the rose garden which had long been his and her aunt's pride and joy.

As she stepped out onto the terrace, the man was still cantering up and down the lawn, with no regard for anyone else. She could not believe his audacity, and she called out to him in what she hoped were forceful terms.

"You there, what do you think you are doing? These gardens are private, how dare you canter your horse across my lawns in such a way. Begone," she said.

At her words, the man pulled up his horse and turned. His appearance quite surprised her. He was not some commoner from the village, not a farmhand or a laborer, but a well-dressed man. She took in his blond hair and had to admit he had a handsome face. Despite the smirk it wore as he dismounted his horse.

"What do you think you are doing?" she repeated as he walked towards her.

"Oh, I am sorry," he said, though his look suggested otherwise.

"Sorry? You have ruined the lawn, look at the hoof marks across it. My gardener shall be most displeased," Madeline said, fixing him with a hard stare.

"*Your* gardener? But I thought Puthall Abbey was home to Victoria Crenshaw, and if I am not mistaken, she is far older than you," he said, smiling at her.

"My aunt is dead," she replied curtly, "and I am mistress of Puthall Abbey now."

"How terrible of me, please forgive me. My name is Stoddard, Wesley Stoddard," and he held out his hand to her. "It is a pleasure to meet you."

Once more, she could swear that a smirk played across his face. Such arrogance would never do.

CHAPTER TWO

*M*adeline took his hand warily and nodded. There was an air of arrogance about him, which she found unpleasant. The fact that he had so brazenly ridden across her lawn suggested he held himself in far higher regard than others ought to.

"A new mistress at Puthall Abbey? Well, it is all change in the district, is it not?" he said, looking up at the house. "I myself have just moved here. I saw your aunt from a distance on several occasions and in church. When I was there, at least." He laughed again.

"My family, the Crenshaws, have been resident at the abbey since the reformation," Madeline replied.

"And you are the next in a long line of inheritors. I did not know your aunt had any family. I was told she was a spinster and something of an eccentric," he replied.

"A few months is hardly long enough to garner any sort of opinion, but still, you thought you would ride across her lawns roughshod and with no regard for anyone else." Madeline knew her anger was rising again.

"I was taking a shortcut home. The horse is an excitable creature, and I can only apologize for his hooves. There is a right of way over the land, I can show you the deeds if you wish." He raised his eyebrows, and Madeline shook her head. "I live across the meadow there, in Puthall House. It is smaller than I am used to, but it will do. For now," he replied, pointing towards the house, which lay through the trees.

As a child, Madeline had always been told to stay away from Puthall House. At that time, it had been home to a most disagreeable gentleman who kept a strange array of animals about the place and was rumored to have a large cat prowling about the lower floors. It seemed that the tradition of unsavory characters at the house continued, and Madeline wished to have as little to do with her neighbor as possible.

"Well ..." she began, "next time you use this 'right of way,' I would ask you to do so without tearing up half the lawn."

"A right of way is a right of way, *Miss* ...?" he said, fixing her with a smile.

"Crenshaw, Madeline Crenshaw, and I would ask you, *Mr.* Stoddard, to take more care in the future," she replied.

"Lord Stoddard, Miss Crenshaw. My family has held a noble title since long before the reformation, our estate is in Sussex. But I have come to Hertfordshire to ... well, enjoy myself. I am sure we will get along just fine as neighbors, and you are always welcome at Puthall House."

Madeline did not extend a similar invitation to Wesley, and the two stood in a somewhat awkward silence for a moment, until Wesley's horse let out an exasperated whinny and stomped its hoof.

"The poor creature is impatient. I suggest you take your right of way and go home," Madeline said, fixing Wesley with a hard stare.

He smiled at her and mounted the horse once more, turning the animal and making to leave.

"You are always welcome at Puthall House, Miss Crenshaw, do not forget it. I am sure we will be the best of friends very soon," he said and cantered off across the lawn.

Madeline watched him go and shook her head. The audacity of the man was quite astonishing, and she could not believe his brazenness and manner of tone. He crossed the lawn and proceeded through the gate at the bottom and over the meadow towards Puthall House. Madeline only turned away when she was certain he was gone. At last, she stepped back inside with a heavy sigh.

"Are you all right, ma'am?" Mrs. Morrison asked. "I was going to send Milton and Robin out to assist you. They would have sent that vagabond packing."

"He is no vagabond, though I should be glad to never see him again. *That* was Lord Wesley Stoddard, our new neighbor," Madeline replied, shaking her head.

"A lord? A new neighbor? At Puthall House? That place has not been let in years. Not since Sir Benedict Pritchard had it, and he has been dead these past ten years. I remember when you were a little girl, you were quite frightened of the place," Mrs. Morrison said, tutting.

"Well, it seems there is a new owner now and one that I am not keen to make further acquaintance with. He says there is a right of way across the lawns and that he will take it when he pleases," Madeline said, as the housekeeper looked at her in surprise.

"The old way to the church, ma'am. But no one has used it in a hundred years. They would not have dared do so when your aunt lived here, God rest her soul. Liberties, ma'am, that is what that man is taking. I doubt he is even a lord. Lord Muck, that is what I shall call him," and she picked up the tea tray and bustled out of the room, muttering to herself.

Madeline was still angry at the way in which Wesley Stoddard had spoken to her. He had hardly expressed any sympathy for the news that her aunt was dead. Nor did he appear to possess any of the manners one would expect from a member of the aristocracy. But she had grown used to such things during her seasons in London and knew that aristocratic rank was hardly a precursor for aristocratic manners. In fact, it was quite the opposite at times.

She resolved there and then to have as little to do with her neighbor as possible. This was her home, and it had been her family's residence for generations. Puthall Abbey was in her blood, and she had every intention of making the place a wonderful home. It was what her aunt would have wanted, and she would have stood no nonsense from anyone, least of all an arrogant minor peer who careered his horse across her lawns.

"Good riddance to him," she said out loud as she made her way from the drawing room, "may he never cross my path again."

CHAPTER THREE

*W*esley Stoddard had been surprised at the appearance of his new neighbor. He had taken a shortcut across the lawns of Puthall Abbey on his return from the village that day, expecting to face little opposition to his route. The right of way was clearly marked, albeit on a rather old map he had found in the library, and his disposition to self-confidence had ensured he possessed no qualms in taking it.

He had not realized that the elderly Victoria Crenshaw was dead, nor that she had a most attractive niece who was to inherit. The observation of Madeline's qualities had been immediate, and despite the icy reception he had been given, he could not help but find the young brunette an attractive proposition.

It was this thought which preoccupied him as he rode across the lawns after their encounter. He paused by the gate and looked back to where Madeline was still standing, watching him leave.

"A spirited girl," he said out loud, as the horse whinnied as though in agreement.

From the gate, he made his way across the meadows towards Puthall House. It was far smaller than the abbey and far smaller than his own Sussex estate, but it was a charming house in its own way. Though over the years, it had fallen into disrepair. Wesley had come there for some rest and recuperation following a short illness, and the beauty of that part of Hertfordshire seemed to suit his temperament well.

The house was set in rambling grounds, and ivy and clematis grew up its sides, almost obscuring many of the windows. Roses rambled about the door, and wisteria hung over the lower windows so that the house appeared almost as an extension of the gardens, rather than master of that which it surveyed. Though, at this time of year, there was a bareness to the place, and the leaves had fallen from the trees. From the door one could just make out Puthall Abbey through the trees, and Wesley was pleased to have made acquaintance with his new neighbor, despite her obvious coldness towards him.

As he rode up to the door of Puthall House, he breathed a satisfied sigh and dismounted, as his loyal valet, Brooks, came to meet him.

"A fine day is it not, Brooks?" he said, stretching out his arms and looking about him.

"Yes, My Lord, a letter has arrived for you. I have placed it in your study," the valet replied, taking his master's coat and hat.

"Very good, very good," Wesley replied absentmindedly as a stable boy took his horse. He had little time for correspondence and had never been good at administration, always leaving things to the last minute or neglecting serious pieces of business that required his attention.

"It had the mark of Mr. Thorne's solicitors, sir," Brooks continued.

At this, Wesley looked up in surprise. He had heard

nothing from his old friend, Milton Thorne, for some months. He'd been on the continent, engaged in one of the many wars which the empire was fighting at that moment, wars which Wesley Stoddard had done his best to avoid.

"Why are his solicitor's writing to me?" Wesley asked, turning in surprise to the valet who shrugged his shoulders.

"I am not sure Your Lordship. I do not make a habit of opening correspondence," the valet replied.

Wesley smiled and nodded. The valet was a loyal man, and Wesley would trust him with his life. He had been with him since he was a boy, and whilst he was outspoken at times, he was also entirely dependable.

"Then I had best see what they want. No doubt I am to act on his behalf once more in some ludicrous business dealing whilst he is off conquering Europe for the crown," Wesley said, strolling into the house.

Despite the bright but chilly day outside, the interior of Puthall House was dark. The shutters were thrown back, but the ivy cladding hung low across the windows, obscuring much of the light. The place was dusty too and in need of a good clean, but Wesley kept only a handful of servants to see to his needs, and there was little time for the rudiments of housework. He minded not though and was quite content to live in the manner he had become accustomed to. The house suited him just fine, and the local legends about its previous occupants ensured that visitors were few and far between.

In his study, which was really nothing but a desk littered with unopened correspondence and lined with unread books, he found the letter. Brooks had placed it on a silver tray, and it was perched on a table by the fire, which remained unlit. Wesley settled himself down and slid the letter opener across the neatly printed envelope. It bore the seal of Straughton and Straughton, Solicitors. They were a city firm that his friend had long used to correspond with him. Usually, when he wanted something official, or something kept quiet. Wesley's connections made him a useful contact, and it would not be the first time that his friend had called upon his services.

. . .

D*ear Lord Stoddard,*

It is my regret to inform you that Captain Milton Thorne of the King's Lancer's and a notable client of this firm, has been killed in action on the continent. The news reached us this morning, and we have corresponded with you immediately.

Wesley sat back in disbelief, the letter held aloft in his hand. His old friend, Milton, dead? He could hardly believe it. The man had always seemed indestructible. Always a part of his life for so many years. They had been at school together, and Wesley could not have imagined anyone braver or more courageous than Milton Thorne.

"Astonishing," he said out loud, shaking his head as he continued to read.

. . .

His funeral has taken place with full military honors behind British lines, he was laid to rest alongside his men. His instructions to this firm at the time of writing his will were that we should have full responsibility for all aspects of his estate, including his daughter, Cornelia.

I write to inform you that since Cornelia has no living relatives, the wishes of her father are that she be placed into your care. You are his oldest friend, and he believes he could trust you, not only with his own life but also with that of his daughter.

I trust that you shall take on this task with the utmost diligence, Your Lordship, and I have made arrangements for Cornelia to travel to Puthall House on the 17th of this month. I trust that this will be acceptable to you. I understand that Captain Thorne discussed the issue in its entirety with you before making his will.

It is with a heavy heart that I bear this news to you. I hope that some happiness will come from it, in the knowledge that Cornelia will enter a happy home and be well cared for.

Please do not hesitate to be in touch with me should

you require further clarification of the details of the will, which also provides a small dowry for Cornelia and the provision of expenses for her keep.

I remain yours, ever,

Granville Straughton, Solicitor.

W esley shook his head, trying to deny the words he had just read. It was impossible, impossible! Not only to learn of the death of his friend, but also of the provisions of Milton's will. His friend had never discussed the possibility of his daughter coming to live with him. Had never mentioned that Wesley should take her should he suffer the sad fate which had now befallen him. It was quite astonishing, and not to mention, rude. Red hot anger surged through Wesley at the thought that he was now to act as guardian to a child. A child he knew nothing of nor desired to know anything of. The last he had heard of Cornelia was that she was in the care of a governess whilst her father went off to war.

"Brooks," he called, ringing the bell for the valet.

The man appeared a moment later.

"Read this."

"My Lord?" Brooks replied, looking at his master in confusion.

"Read it," Wesley said, quite forgetting any sorrow he had felt in the learning of Milton's death.

The valet took the letter and read through it, his eyebrows rising as he did so.

"But, My Lord. Today is the seventeenth of the month. The child must be on her way here now," he said, as Wesley threw his hands up in exasperation and let out a cry.

"A child? Here? I cannot have a child here. I am no parent. I know nothing about such things. He did not consult me on the matter, and now I am to have her here under my care. It is an impropriety of the highest order." Wesley was shaking his head and looking down at the letter again in disbelief, as Brooks handed it back.

"Shall I have the maids make up a room for the girl?" Brooks asked, in his usual matter of fact tone.

"A room? But... I have not even agreed to it. And she will need... need things, items, whatever a child needs. All of which we do not possess for I have never cared for a child, nor do I wish to do so," he said, his frustration growing as he began to pace up and down the room.

"My Lord, if the child is on her way, then we must take her in. You can hardly send her back to London to sit on the steps of the solicitor's," Brooks replied.

"And why not? It is they who sent her, she can jolly well return to them. I am not her ward," Wesley replied.

He was incensed by his friend's audacity and intended having nothing to do with the child. She could go back to her governess. He would arrange a school for her, perhaps, paid for by her father's estate, but after that, he had no sense of responsibility to her. The child was an orphan, and her father should have made proper provision for her.

"According to this letter, you are, My Lord," Brooks said, tilting his head to one side, "and if I am not mistaken, the sounds of a carriage come from outside.

You can hardly send a little girl who has just lost her father back to London, can you?"

Wesley grimaced. The sounds of a carriage could indeed be heard coming from outside, and a moment later there was a knock at the door.

"She... oh, heavens. Very well, tell the maid to make up a room for her. Come now, let us see what the child is like. I hope she is quiet and well behaved. I want as little to do with her as possible, is that understood?" Wesley said, following the valet into the hallway.

"It is, My Lord," Brookes replied, and he opened the door.

In front of them stood a young girl of no more than eleven years old. She looked warily up at Wesley, the merest hint of a tear in her eye. Behind her stood a tall man with a disagreeable looking wig perched on his head.

"Lord Stoddard? Horace Straughton, Captain Thorne's solicitor. You have received the letter from my brother, I presume?" the man said, scratching the side of his head and fixing Wesley with a smile.

"Just this morning," Wesley replied, eyeing Cornelia with suspicion.

She made no response, her stare unblinking and making him feel quite uncomfortable. He had no natural affinity with children and with no nieces or nephews, or even distant cousins, he had had little practice in dealing with anyone of a young age since he himself was so afflicted. His own childhood had been difficult, owing to his often-absent mother and overbearing father. She would often take to her bed for days on end, complaining of a minor ailment. The late Lord Stoddard would be far too busy dealing with affairs of state to pay any attention to his son. On the odd occasion that he did so, he would simply remind the young Wesley to behave like a man and not put a foot out of line. Childhood was something he wished to forget, and he resented the living embodiment of it now stood before him.

"Ah, very good. Then you will know that Cornelia is to reside with you until she is of age to inherit her father's fortune," the solicitor replied, pushing Cornelia over the threshold and never failing in his fixed smile.

"I have had that fact communicated to me, yes," he

replied, still looking the girl up and down with some disbelief.

"And you have made the proper provisions for her?" Mr. Straughton continued.

"I ... well ..." Wesley began.

"Splendid, then I shall leave her in your capable hands, Lord Stoddard. You really are a very kind gentleman, and I am sure young Cornelia here will be very happy," the solicitor said, and with a nod of his head, he turned back towards the carriage.

"I say, what about the money for her upkeep?" Wesley called after him.

"My brother will be in touch," came the reply, and Mr. Straughton was shortly back in his carriage, his task completed as Wesley's began.

"Well now, do you not come with a governess?" Wesley asked, looking down at Cornelia, who fixed him with a sullen look. She shook her head.

"Just a bag, My Lord," Brooks said, taking up the small traveling case at Cornelia's side.

"And school? Do you go to school? I presume

someone will come to collect you. A boarding school, so you will only remain here at Puthall House a while?" Wesley said, attempting to jolly himself up. Again, she shook her head.

"Shall I have the housekeeper ask around for a tutor for the girl?" Brooks asked, clearly finding some amusement in the situation.

"No, Brooks, you shall not. Young lady, you will only remain here for a short time. I am sorry for the loss of your father. He was a good friend to me, at least he was before ... anyway, I shall see to it that a suitable school is found for you and you shall be sent there. It does no harm to a child to be sent away to school," he said, as much for his own benefit as hers.

Cornelia remained silent, and the three stood awkwardly in the hallway for some moments. Wesley had no idea what to say next, and he sighed, tilting his head to one side and looking at the young girl in a state of utter disbelief. What could he possibly offer her as a parent? The whole thing was ludicrous, and he wished as little to do with her as possible. She'd be sent away to school by the end of the week, and that would be that.

"My Lord?" Brooks said, some moments later as the silence continued to reign heavy upon them.

"Show this young lady to her room and see to it she has something to eat," Wesley said.

"Her room, sir?" Brooks asked.

"Yes, Brooks. The room that has been prepared for her ..." Wesley replied.

"Ah, of course. And will the young lady dine with you this evening, sir?" the valet continued.

"With me? No, she will not, is there no nursery in this house? She may dine with the maids or alone, as is her wish. Now, I want no further disturbances. Am I understood?" Wesley said, and Brooks bowed.

"Of course, My Lord. Fully. This way, young lady," he said, placing his hand on Cornelia's shoulder and finding himself unable to suppress a smile.

Wesley watched them go with a grimace upon his face. What an awful day this had turned into. He could not possibly be responsible for the girl; it was ludicrous. He returned to his study, where he wrote a strongly worded letter of protest to Mr. Straughton. In it, he listed all the reasons why he was entirely unsuitable to be the girl's guardian and that at the next available opportunity the solicitors were to come and collect her. Until then, Wesley would decide upon a school for her, and there she would remain. Occasional visits would be permitted, but he had no intention of Cornelia becoming a permanent fixture about his person. But as he sealed the envelope, he could not help but feel that his protest would fall on deaf ears. It was a rotten trick of Milton's to write him into his will in that manner, without even consulting him. Anger was replaced with sadness. He presumed his friend had no expectation of the imminent death which had befallen him.

Wesley sighed and got up to look out of the window. His study faced the meadows and looked across to Puthall Abbey beyond. Life had seemed much simpler this morning when he was arguing with Miss Crenshaw as to rights of way across her land. It had all got rather complicated now, and he wondered just what the future held.

"She cannot possibly remain here," he said out loud, tutting loudly, "I am as ill-suited to parenting as Miss Crenshaw is to good manners. Perhaps I should send the child trespassing in the gardens of Puthall Abbey, she is welcome to her."

He poured himself a brandy and sat back in the chair by the unlit fire. This would not do at all. A child? At Puthall House? It was like a nightmare, but as he sipped his brandy Wesley knew it to be all too real and that what he did next could well change his life forever.

CHAPTER FOUR

*A*fter the encounter with her new neighbor, Madeline did not venture out of Puthall Abbey for several days. There was much to do in the house and a lifetime of her aunt's possessions to sort through. Despite spending so many happy childhood days there, Madeline had seen only half of the house. She spent several mornings exploring the upper rooms and discovering staircases and corridors that she did not even know existed.

"I had not realized there is a suite in the left wing with such exquisite decorations, the wallpaper is remarkable," Madeline said, as Mrs. Morrison served her morning tea a few days later.

"The peacock suite, ma'am? Oh, yes, it was

decorated for the arrival of Queen Anne, or so they say. She only stayed one night, but then that is what you do for royalty, I suppose," the housekeeper replied.

Madeline smiled and took a slice of cake from the plate which Agatha proffered. She had a box of her aunt's correspondence open and was undertaking the dull task of filing unpaid bills and settling accounts. Her aunt was a lavish spender, and unfortunately, there had been times when her lavish income had still not met the expenses she had incurred.

"There will need to be some tightening of the belt, Agatha. At least until these debts are paid off," Madeline said, as the housekeeper fussed about the room with her duster.

"I shall tell Mrs. Fowler to order mutton from now on and to skip the Charlotte Russe this evening," the housekeeper replied.

"Well, let us not go mad, Agatha. A few economies here and there would not hurt, though," Madeline replied, raising her eyebrow at a bill for two dozen bottles of claret, as yet unpaid.

"Will that be all, ma'am? I could do with a nice cup of tea myself, I think," the housekeeper said, and Madeline nodded.

"Yes, thank you. I must take a walk. I have been stuck indoors for too long these past few days. I thought perhaps I might call upon Miss Davies, she was always a good friend to my aunt. I would like to give her something to remember her by. I have found out a necklace inlaid with pearls. It is a beautiful piece, and I am sure she would like it," Madeline said.

"Oh, dear old Alice. She will be pleased to see you. She is getting on in years, though I guess none of us are getting any younger." Mrs. Morrison nodded to Madeline as she left the room.

Madeline laid aside the pile of bills and put on her bonnet. It was a pleasant day outside, a warm breeze was blowing across the gardens. She gazed across to Puthall House, wondering what its occupier was doing that day. Despite herself, she had developed something of a lurid fascination for him. He intrigued her, as arrogant and brazen as he was. Who was he behind the bluster? And why had he chosen Puthall to make his retreat to? She had no wish to encounter him, and took the long way around to the village, passing by the church with its tall steeple from which the bell was just striking three.

Alice Davies lived in a pretty cottage with roses around the door. It stood just outside the village in its own grounds. Madeline had often visited the elderly widow with her aunt. They would take tea in the garden during the summer, surrounded by roses and lavender in which the bees buzzed, and butterflies flapped. Madeline had fond memories of Alice. She found her in the garden, almost exactly as she had pictured her, deadheading her late-blooming plants.

"My dear, Madeline. I wondered when I might see you, come and sit down inside," she said, pointing towards the open door of the house.

"I am so glad to see you, and I am sorry not to have come sooner. There seems to be endless little tasks to perform about the house. My aunt has left me something of a legacy to sort out," Madeline replied as they stepped inside, and a maid appeared bearing a tea tray.

"Your aunt's administration skills always left something to be desired," Alice said, laying aside her secateurs and the basket of deadheads before joining Madeline at the tea table.

"There just seems to be so much to sort out," Madeline said, shaking her head.

"You will have it all in hand in no time, my dear. I am certain of that. I am just pleased that you have taken on the job. I had wondered if the excitement of London might hold you for a few more years," Alice said.

"Oh, no, the excitement of London is well past, I can assure you of that. Give me the country any day, though perhaps not with every neighbor I have thus far encountered," Madeline replied.

At this, Alice smiled and nodded her head knowingly.

"Ahh! Do you mean Lord Stoddard? The new tenant at Puthall House? I have already had a run in with him myself. He has objected to the ringing of the church bells. Apparently, it disturbs his sleep, though I can hardly imagine that the sound carries all the way to Puthall House," she said, laughing.

"He thought it his right to ride his horse across the lawns of the abbey and then had the audacity to tell me that it was a right of way, enshrined upon some ancient map he had found. He is quite the rudest man I have ever met, and I have met some rude men," Madeline said, taking a sip of tea and a slice of seed cake.

"He came up to me after church on Sunday. One of the rare occasions since his arrival that he has bothered to make an appearance at the divine service. Quite why I should have any responsibility for the bells is beyond me. Anyway, he launched into an absurd tirade. It was almost laughable, and in the end, he wished me a good morning and walked off. I think that perhaps beneath it all, there is a good man," Alice said, smiling at Madeline, who raised her eyebrows.

"He is certainly an interesting character, though I cannot see what you could find good about him?"

Alice laughed. "I feel he is bored and is hiding some feelings under his manner. Despite it all, I felt as if he was having fun rather than trying to cause offense."

Madeline shook her head. "Still, I have no wish to encounter him again anytime soon."

"When you are neighbors in a small village like Puthall, it seems inevitable. I remember Mrs. Peterson, a woman who lived in the cottage opposite. Your Aunt Victoria could not stand her. They had fallen out years ago over some silly tryst or other. They both refused to speak to the other. It was always most amusing watching your aunt arrive, if Mrs. Peterson saw her, she would rush indoors and slam the door, and your aunt would cross the street to avoid her. They never made their peace, though perhaps you saw her on the day of your aunt's funeral? She was sitting at the back of the church, and there was a tear in her eye. Sometimes the people we dislike the most can, in fact, be amongst the ones we miss the greatest in our lives. It is a funny old world," Alice said, shaking her head.

"Well, in the case of Lord Stoddard and I, if I see him tearing across the lawns again, I shall give him a piece of my mind," Madeline said, laughing.

"It sounds as though you already have," Alice replied and chuckled.

The two women sat enjoying one another's company for much of the afternoon. Alice was delighted with the necklace and promised to wear it on the first possible occasion. Madeline was pleased to have visited her aunt's friend. In her mannerisms, she reminded her so much of Vicky. As they bid one another farewell, she promised to return soon to take tea in the garden.

"Or perhaps I shall call upon you at the abbey. I do love the old place so very much. I am glad it is now in your care," Alice said, as she kissed Madeline on the cheek and watched her depart.

Madeline assured her she was always welcome. As she left, she was not ready to return home just yet, and she found herself taking a path which she and her aunt often used. It was one which took her through Bluebell Woods and along a path leading into the abbey's gardens. It was a cold and crisp day, and a robin was chirping in the bare trees above. It had not taken Madeline long to know that Puthall was her home. The delights of London, if that is what they may be called, held no sway for her. She was happy here, though she missed her aunt dreadfully. There was an emptiness to the house, one which would take some getting used to. As she walked, she could hear her aunt's words of advice upon the matter.

"Find a husband, dear," but Madeline had no interest in such things.

She was far happier in her own company or that of friends like Alice. As she walked along, she resolved to fill Puthall Abbey with friends, visitors from town, and old acquaintances. Their presence would help bring the abbey alive, and it seemed the perfect antidote to any sort of melancholy which might hang over her. She paused to breathe in the scent of the woodland and plucked a posy of early snowdrops to put in a vase in the drawing room. She had always loved flowers, the sight of which brought her much happiness and delight.

She had just tied the posy carefully with her handkerchief when a sound from along the path caused her to look up. If she had not thought herself to be quite alone, then she would have sworn that she could hear a child crying through the trees. Looking around, she could see no one, just the sun casting its rays through the bare canopy of branches above and beyond that the surrounding countryside. But there it was again.

This time it was undeniably a child's cry, low and plaintive, and as she walked tentatively along the track, it became more pronounced. Somewhere, a child was crying, and Madeline was filled with sorrow at the sound of its distress.

"Hello?" she called out, looking about her.

The child's crying ceased, and Madeline called out again but received no reply.

"It is all right, do show yourself. My name is Madeline. I should hate to think of a child crying all alone in these beautiful woods," she said, still looking around her for the source of the sound.

A moment later, there stepped from the trees a pretty little girl, whose face, however, was stained with tears. Her dress was messy from having sat upon the forest floor. She looked scared and peered anxiously at Madeline, as though expecting some sort of chastisement.

"Well, hello there, what a pretty little thing you are. Why are you out here all alone?" Madeline asked, taking a few steps towards the girl who backed away.

"It is all right, there is nothing to be frightened of.

Perhaps an easier question then, what is your name? I am Madeline," she said, smiling at the little girl who continued to stare nervously at her.

"I ... my name is Cornelia," the little girl eventually said, and Madeline knelt on the ground so that their eyes were level.

"Well, that is a very pretty name and one you should be proud of. And now that we both know one another's names, we are strangers no longer and can be friends. Perhaps you can tell me why you are crying? It is far too nice a day to be sat crying, do you not think?" Madeline said.

She could not for the life of her think why a little girl so well dressed should be out in Bluebell Woods all alone. What a terrible thing it was, and she would see to it that the child was reunited with its parents.

"I ... I ran away," the girl said and promptly burst into tears.

adeline was almost in tears herself at the sight of the poor little girl who hung her head before her with tears rolling down her cheeks. Whatever could such a young thing have to run away from? Instinctively, she stepped forward and put her arm around Cornelia and held her close to her.

"There, there, you poor thing. Is there anything I can do to help?"

The child just stared at the ground.

"I cannot just leave you out here in the woods all alone. It will start to grow dark soon. Then you will never find your way. Will you tell me what is wrong?" Madeline asked, taking out her handkerchief and offering it to the little girl.

The child dabbed her eyes and nodded. "I ... I just wish my father was still alive. I miss him so very much. He was so brave and courageous, but he was killed, and my mother is dead too. I am all alone in the world, except for a guardian whom I detest and whom it seems detests me too," she said, the last words sounding ever so forceful as she burst into a fresh flood of tears.

"You poor thing, come now. We cannot stand out here in the woods all afternoon. Do you know my house? Puthall Abbey? We can go there, and my housekeeper will bring us tea and hot buttered teacakes. Would you like that? Then we can talk a little more, you do not have to run away. I am sure I can help you," Madeline said, taking Cornelia by the hand.

How terrible it was to find such an innocent creature all alone out here. Madeline shuddered to think what might have happened if she had remained in the woods during the night. As they arrived back at the abbey, Mrs. Morrison looked surprised to see the child holding Madeline's hand and fixed them with a puzzled look.

"Ma'am, is everything all right? Where has this child come from?" she asked, laying down her duster.

"I found her in Bluebell Woods, she says she is running away, though from whom I am yet to discover. Will you bring us some tea, Agatha, and a mound of hot buttered tea cakes," Madeline asked.

"I will, ma'am, and a piece of Cook's special fruit cake too. I am yet to meet a child who does not like Cook's special fruit cake. You adored it when you were her age," Mrs. Morrison replied, patting Cornelia on the head.

"I remember it well, thank you, Agatha. Now then, Cornelia, you come with me to the drawing room, and we shall make you comfortable," Madeline said.

She seated the little girl on a sofa near the fire. She was quiet now, her tears all dried up and a sad expression upon her face. Presently, Mrs. Morrison appeared again, this time with a silver tray bearing all manner of delectable teatime treats.

"She looks like she could do with a good feeding,

though her dress is of the finest quality," Mrs. Morrison whispered to Madeline, as she poured the tea.

Madeline nodded and placed the plate of teacakes in front of Cornelia. The child began to eat hungrily. Madeline watched her with curiosity. It did seem odd that she was so nicely dressed yet also so evidently neglected. As she finished her third teacake, Madeline cleared her throat and took a sip of tea.

"So, Cornelia, will you tell me something about yourself? If I am to help you, then I must know who your guardian is. Perhaps they are looking for you. Did you tell anyone of your plan to run away?" Madeline asked, in what she hoped was a soothing and reassuring tone.

Cornelia shook her head.

"I only left an hour ago, no one will have noticed. They do not care about me, *he* just wants to send me off to boarding school as soon as possible. He will be glad I am gone, and I am glad that I will not see him again," Cornelia said, taking another large bite of teacake followed by a mouthful of fruit cake.

Madeline was curious to know who this wicked man was. Apart from Puthall House and the abbey, there were no large houses to speak of in the immediate vicinity. It seemed unlikely that the kindly Sir Robert Riding of Hartmier Manor should treat one of his granddaughters so cruelly. Besides, he prided himself upon the fact that he engaged a tutor who had once taught at the royal court. A fact which he had bored her aunt with on every occasion of their meeting. Could she be the daughter of a tenant farmer? In which case, Madeline would review the tenancy in the light of such cruelty.

"But ... who is this guardian? He seems quite the wicked man. Why are you under his care?"

The child would not answer.

"I am new in this inheritance, but I never heard my Aunt Vicky speak of a little girl living nearby. Did you ever meet her?" Madeline asked.

Cornelia shook her head through a mouthful of fruitcake, and a tear ran down her cheek.

"I only arrived here a few days ago. My father died only a few weeks past, and as soon as his will was read, it instructed that I should come here into the care of ..." she said, beginning to sob again.

"Into the care of whom?" Madeline asked.

"Lord Stoddard," Cornelia said, almost dropping her plate as she began to weep uncontrollably.

So much for Alice Davies' assessment that beneath the rudeness and arrogance of Wesley Stoddard there lurked a good man, Madeline thought to herself. She had disliked her neighbor at first, but now she despised him for his treatment of the poor creature sitting before her.

"Lord Stoddard? He is your guardian? Then you have drawn an unlucky lot, my dear Cornelia, an unlucky lot indeed," Madeline said, shaking her head.

"He intends to send me away to boarding school. It is all he speaks of whenever he sets eyes upon me. I hate him, he is so cold and unkind. I eat alone in the nursery and have no one to talk to except Brooks, the valet. That is why I ran away, I never want to see him again," Cornelia said, her face screwed into an angry expression.

"You must not worry, dear. I shall speak to Lord Stoddard, he has no right to treat you like that. Be assured that I understand how you feel, I lost my own parents when I was young, and the only person I had was my dear Aunt Vicky. Now she is gone, and so perhaps you and I can be friends, would you like that?" Madeline asked, coming to sit next to Cornelia on the sofa.

The young girl nodded and smiled weakly at Madeline, who patted her hand. At that moment, Mrs. Morrison appeared, bearing yet more hot buttered teacakes fresh from the oven.

"Ah, Agatha. Would you sit with Cornelia, please? I must pay a social call to Lord Stoddard," Madeline said, wrapping her shawl around her.

"To Lord Stoddard, ma'am?" the housekeeper said, laying down the tray and wiping her hands on her apron.

"Yes, it turns out that he is Cornelia's guardian, and it is he who has so mistreated her so as to cause her to run away," Madeline replied.

"So, it is not just lawns he has no respect for," the housekeeper said, raising her eyebrows, "I will sit with her, ma'am, but I would not expect much from His Lordship. Not after the way he behaved the other day."

"We shall see, now take good care of her, Mrs. Morrison. I shall be back shortly," Madeline said, opening the doors onto the terrace.

"We shall have a jolly time together and finish these teacakes," Mrs. Morrison said, taking one of the freshly buttered treats, as Madeline stepped outside.

Dusk was falling now, and she hurried across the lawn towards the gate leading into the meadow. Her anger was rising against Wesley Stoddard. It was one thing to behave in a rude and abrasive manner towards one's neighbor, but quite another to mistreat a child in such an appalling way. Cornelia appeared a sweet little thing, and why anyone should wish to pack her off to boarding school and be rid of her was quite beyond Madeline's comprehension.

As she approached the house, her pace slowed. It was almost dark now, a few solitary candles burned in the windows. She remembered the stories from her childhood, about the strange animals which the previous owner had kept there. She had never seen them of course, but village rumor listed everything from a lion to snakes and birds which answered back when they were spoken to.

"Do not be so silly," she said to herself, pulling her shawl about her.

She would knock on the door and tell Lord Stoddard just what she thought of him. It was no way to treat a little girl and particularly one who had lost so much. Madeline thought back to that sad moment in her own childhood when the news had arrived at Puthall Abbey of her own dear father's death on the battlefield. Her aunt had taken her into the drawing room and explained it through a tear-stained face. Mrs. Morrison had made a strong tea with sugar and put her to bed. How awful it must be for Cornelia to have no one like Aunt Vicky to comfort her. Madeline had already resolved to inform Lord Stoddard that she would gladly take responsibility for the poor child if only to save her from his careless ways.

There was no one about at the front of the house, but

the imposing door was slightly ajar and from beyond, a slither of candlelight flickered out into the darkness. Madeline reminded herself not to be so silly as to think that prowling beasts and other eccentricities might still be lurking inside. It was a strange house, almost like a plant, rising from the ground, for the ivy was so thick and dense about it. The scent of roses and wisteria hung in the air, for despite the darkness, it was still a warm evening, and above her, an owl hooted, causing her to startle.

"Hello?" she called out tentatively, but there was no answer.

She pushed open the door to reveal the hallway beyond. Two candles burned on the mantelpiece above the fireplace, where a measly few sticks were crackling in the hearth. There was no warmth to them, and the hallway felt colder than the outside.

"Hello?" she called again, a little louder this time, and she half expected Wesley to jump out on her in some vicious prank.

But there was no one around. As she stepped further into the hallway, she could hear voices coming from some distant room. They were muffled. It was impossible to tell precisely what they were saying. She was sure she heard Cornelia's name mentioned, and instead of calling out again, she crept through the house to the source of the noise, listening lest she should be discovered.

The voice was unmistakably that of Wesley Stoddard. She arrived outside what she presumed to be his study. The corridor was dark, but from beneath the door, there came a chink of light and the replies of another voice she did not recognize, though she presumed it must be that of the valet, Brooks.

They were talking in raised voices, arguing over something. As she pressed her ear to the door, she heard the name Cornelia again, followed by a curse, which she herself would never repeat. How awful this man was! She had a good mind to set him straight on several matters... firstly, his ill-treatment of his ward.

"I will not allow him to get away with this," she said to herself, and taking a deep breath, she prepared to open the door.

CHAPTER SIX

Wesley Stoddard had been lounging in his study for most of the afternoon. The doors out into the garden were flung wide open, and a cool breeze was coming in from outside. It was a pleasant enough day, or at least it would've been had he not had the worry of his young ward playing on his mind. It had been several days since Cornelia had arrived at Puthall House, and Wesley had sought as little to do with her as possible. It was not that she was rude or difficult, nor was she badly behaved or inclined to answer back, she was just a little girl and herein lay the problem. Wesley had no experience of such things, and he found her presence unsettling. He could not be a parent to her, nor did he have much in the way of comfort for her over the loss of her father. In short, he was entirely out of his depth and had already prepared inquiries to various notable public schools as to her education. It seemed the best thing for all involved, especially for her. What could she gain from him?

"But schooling is for boys, My Lord," Brooks had told him as Wesley had issued instructions as to where the letters should be sent.

"But surely the notable public schools will accept girls? Eton, Harrow, Rugby?" he had replied.

"No, My Lord. They will not. Young ladies are expected to be educated at home by a governess. There is little call for women to better themselves. She should be taught French, sewing, the pianoforte, and drawing, and perhaps a little formal etiquette. But that should be the extent of it," Brooks had said, shaking his head and causing Wesley to scowl.

Would he ever be rid of her? Or would the presence of Cornelia continue to follow him about until she came of age? It was a most detestable situation. He had spent much of the afternoon brooding over its resolution. With no tangible results forthcoming, he had poured himself a brandy, despite it only being three o'clock and settled himself down to doze in the hope that there would be no unwelcome disturbances. He was just nodding off when there came a knock at the door and an urgent voice calling to him from the corridor.

"My Lord, My Lord, the girl is missing," came Brooks' voice.

Wesley sighed, could no one control the child? She was hardly a handful. All she had done since her arrival at Puthall House was to mope about looking miserable and eat barely half of what she was given.

"Come in, Brooks," he called, and the door opened revealing the valet in a state of excitement.

"My Lord, the girl is missing. The maid has just been up to the nursery with some tea for her, and she is nowhere to be seen," Brooks said, a worried look upon his face.

"She has probably just gone outside, have you looked in the rose garden? Or in the ornamental garden by the pond? There is all manner of hiding places in a house this size," Wesley replied, with none of the urgency which the valet appeared to wish.

"We have looked, sir. She is nowhere about, and we have been calling for her for some time. I thought Your Lordship would wish to know, given that she is under *your care*," Brooks replied, emphasizing his last words and causing Wesley to sigh.

"Very well, I shall come and assist. But I am sure she has not gone far if indeed she has really disappeared. Where would she go? In a village this size, there is hardly ample opportunity for escape, and it is not as though she is being ill-treated. I realize she does not wish to be here, no more than I wish her to be. But that is how it is for now, and I suppose we must all accept it," he replied.

"It would be no surprise if she has run away, My Lord. You have hardly been welcoming to her," Brooks said. Tutting to himself as he followed Wesley from the room.

"I would remind you with whom you are speaking to, Brooks. You may have been in my employ these many years past, but that does not mean you can speak your mind as you wish," Wesley said, fixing Brooks with an angry stare.

But the words of his valet rang true, and Wesley

knew that what he said was right. He had spoken barely a few words to Cornelia since her arrival, and those had been entirely perfunctory. They had not dined together, nor had he invited her to sit with him in the evenings, preferring his own company instead. In short, he had been entirely lacking towards her and had shown absolutely no sign of affection or welcome to the grieving little girl who now appeared to be missing. It made him feel rather shabby.

"We shall mount a search of the house and grounds," Wesley said. They were standing in the hallway now. Several of the servants had gathered to assist in looking for Cornelia whom no amount of calling had brought forth.

"We have checked all over the house, My Lord," one of the maids said.

"Well, check again, and in the wardrobes and cupboards. She may simply have fallen asleep somewhere. It has been a warm day, and children are prone to such things," he said, having no real idea what children were and were not prone to at all.

Outside, he and Brooks began to search the gardens, calling to Cornelia as they went. There was no sign of her amongst the deadheaded roses, nor in the ornamental garden by the pond. She was not in the orchard. They even checked each tree to see if she were hiding above. After much calling and hunting in the most obscure places, it was agreed amongst the two that Cornelia was missing, and they returned to the house where the housemaid told a similar tale.

"This is frightfully inconvenient," Wesley said, shaking his head.

"For whom, My Lord?" Brooks replied.

"For me, of course," Wesley replied, scowling at the valet, who raised his eyebrows.

"And not for the little girl? Heaven knows where she might be, she could be lost in the woods or worse. If she has made for London, then she could already be part of a traveling circus or picked up by tinkers," Brooks said.

"Well ... oh, darn it, I need time to think," Wesley said, and leaving Brooks and the other servants in the hallway, he stormed off to his study.

This was all too much. He had expected Puthall House to provide the rest and recuperation he needed and not to add to his already considerable burdens, at least as he viewed them. He poured himself a brandy and slumped again in an armchair by the unlit fire. It was beginning to grow dark now, twilight descending upon the gardens, and through the windows, he could see the bats fluttering about the house. It was all too much, and he closed his eyes, allowing the fatigue of the day to wash over him. He had just dozed off when there came a knock at the door and the sound of Brooks' voice calling once more from the corridor

"Supper, My Lord. I presume you still wish to eat despite the situation we find ourselves in."

"Yes, yes, come in," Wesley replied, still disliking his valet's tone.

Brooks was bearing a tray upon which a plate of bread and cheese and a glass of claret was placed, and he set it down, closing the door behind him. Wesley sighed and prepared himself for further chastisement.

"Is there any news of Cornelia?" he asked, hoping that perhaps by some miracle, she had been found.

"None, sir. She is still missing, and the maid which

the housekeeper sent down to the village in search of her has returned with no news," Brooks replied.

"What does one do in such circumstances?" Wesley asked, taking the plate from the tray and settling back in his chair.

"One tends to avoid losing one's ward in the first place, My Lord," Brooks replied.

"Oh, darn it, Brooks. I did not ask for a ward, did I? She has been thrust upon me, upon us, and now I am supposed to be the one to take care of her. I know nothing of her; for all I know she has been planning this all along. You hear of such things," Wesley said, though, in truth, he never had done.

The truth was that he was entirely out of his depth, and now that it was growing dark, he feared privately for Cornelia's safety. Up until now, he had expected that she would come back. That she was having a game with them, but she was only a child, and it worried him that she was out and all alone. He pushed such thoughts aside as he had always been taught. Children were to be suffered, that was what his father had taught him. This was inconvenient; it would be he, Lord Stoddard, who would be the subject of scandalous gossip if anything untoward happened to her. Once again, he cursed Milton. Why had he done such a foolish thing? Despite his lack of judgment in this matter, the man had always been a good friend. He evidently believed Wesley to be his, otherwise he would never have trusted his daughter to him in this way. It looked like that trust had been sorely misplaced.

"We will keep looking, sir. Perhaps if she has run away and is hiding somewhere nearby, a night out in the cold will remind her of the comforts of home," Brooks said, shaking his head.

"If she has not returned by the morning, then we must inform the local militia. They can begin something of a wider search. A child traveling alone is bound to attract attention, she is a pretty thing, despite her sullenness and ..." Wesley said, but he was interrupted by the opening, without invitation, of his study door.

"I have heard quite enough, Lord Stoddard," Madeline said, her face flushed with anger and a defiant look in her eyes.

Wesley could not believe the sight before him. How

dare his neighbor come bursting in unannounced like this?

"I ... I beg your pardon? How dare you. This is my house, and I shall ask you to leave immediately," he replied, looking her up and down with disdain.

"I dare, just as you did when you trampled all over my lawns on your horse," Madeline said, standing before him with her hands upon her hips.

"That was entirely different, and besides, you are interrupting a most important matter. My ward, Cornelia, is missing and we are searching for her," Wesley replied, as Madeline shook her head.

"Yes, I know. I have known all afternoon that she is missing. I found the poor girl crying in Bluebell Woods. How could you be so heartless towards her?" Madeline said.

Now, Wesley really was confused, and his anger was rising at the thought that they had searched high and low for the girl when all along his neighbor had known just where she was.

"You... you knew? You found her? And you thought better of it than to bring her home?" Wesley said, laying aside his plate and rising to face Madeline, who clearly had no intention of backing down.

"Home? To this sorry place and to a guardian who has done nothing but make her feel unwelcome since her arrival? She is perfectly safe at Puthall Abbey, of that I can assure you. We took tea together, she was hungry and desperate for comfort and sympathy, the girl just lost her father!" Madeline replied.

"Hungry? She is well-fed, but she sends half her food back without touching it," Wesley said, recovering somewhat from his surprise at this confrontation.

Brooks was standing quietly in the corner, he shook his head and sighed.

"My Lord, perhaps the girl needs more than just sustenance; a kind word along with it can go a long way," he began.

"I do not require your advice, Brooks," Wesley said, turning angrily to the valet, who bowed and backed away.

"The poor child told me that you intended to send her away to school at the first opportunity. And that you have done nothing to make her welcome or to comfort her following the death of her father. It is outrageous, you are a terrible man," Madeline said.

"I did not ask for this responsibility. Cornelia would have been far better off with a governess in London than sent out here to me. I am no parent; I know nothing of children. But I am grateful to you for finding her, and I shall come at once to collect her, or rather Brooks will go," Wesley said, scowling at his valet.

"She has no desire to return to you. She would only run away again and faced with such an unwelcoming home and guardian I can hardly blame her," Madeline said.

"I ... you ..." Wesley clenched his fists in frustration, though he could hardly disagree with Madeline's assessment of the situation. He was also rather relieved that the girl had been found. What would he have done if he allowed something to happen to her?

"Cornelia may stay with me. She needs to be properly looked after and comforted. No one it seems has done so thus far. She has lost her father in the most traumatic of circumstances, and it is only natural that she should need proper care and attention rather than the terrible treatment she has received here at your hands," Madeline said.

"You have no right to the child. It is to me that her father entrusted her," Wesley said, shaking with anger and wagging his finger at Madeline, who appeared entirely unmoved by his emotions.

"And you have broken that trust, Lord Stoddard. Now, I assure you that Cornelia is perfectly safe and will be well looked after not only by me but also by my household. If you can prove yourself a changed man, then Cornelia herself may make the decision as to where she resides. She will not be sent away from Puthall Abbey, and I would urge you to reconsider the way you are treating her." Madeline turned on her heel and marched from the room, slamming the door behind her.

"But ..." Wesley said, and he slammed his fist down on the mantelpiece, "... what a day."

"My Lord ..." Brooks began, but Wesley turned to him with a sigh.

"I ... am I really as terrible as Miss Crenshaw has implied? I have done nothing to mistreat the child. I am simply not used to the ways of children. Surely, I am not so horrible as to have neglected her emotions?" he asked.

But Brooks made no reply, and taking up the tray, he left his master's study. Wesley slumped back into his chair and put his head into his hands. He had been entrusted with the child, and he had broken that trust, the trust which Milton Thorne had placed in him. It was all such a mess, and in the middle of it was Cornelia, who had done nothing wrong except being the victim of circumstance. Wesley poured himself another brandy and swilled the liquid around in its glass, contemplating the day's events.

"Am I really that terrible?" he said out loud, but the answer he gave himself was far from what he wanted to hear.

CHAPTER SEVEN

Madeline wasted no time returning to Puthall Abbey. It was pitch dark now, but she bravely made her way across the meadows towards the lights burning in the windows of her new home. She was shaking with anger at the audacity and meanness of Lord Stoddard. To think that he could treat Cornelia in such an abysmal way and show no regard for her welfare stunned her. He had behaved like a man who has lost a possession and desires it back. Well, Madeline had no intention of returning Cornelia to him. Not until the child wished to go, and she doubted that would ever be the case.

As she slipped through the terrace doors and into the

drawing room, Mrs. Maddison raised her finger to her lips and pointed to Cornelia, who was fast asleep on the chaise lounge.

"She fell asleep almost as soon as you left, ma'am," the housekeeper said, shaking her head sadly.

"Then she must be left to sleep, put a blanket over her," Madeline replied softly, and the two women made Cornelia comfortable whilst all the while she slept on.

A little while later, they stepped out into the hallway, and Madeline shook her head sadly, a tear in her eye.

"Did you see His Lordship, ma'am?" Agatha asked, and Madeline nodded.

"I saw him, and I have never encountered a more cruel or heartless man in all my life. He cares not for the child at all and is only interested in how soon he can rid himself of her. I have insisted that she remain here for now, despite his objections. We will look after her here at Puthall Abbey and do a far better job of it than Wesley Stoddard," Madeline said

That evening she took her supper alone, and the footmen carried Cornelia up to bed in chambers adjoining Madeline's. The child was exhausted and hardly stirred as the men carried her, and Madeline kissed her goodnight.

"It will be all right, Cornelia, dear," Madeline whispered, and she left her alone to sleep.

Over the coming days, Madeline sought to discover more about Cornelia, but she was ever watchful for signs of Wesley Stoddard returning to claim his ward. She heard nothing from him, though, and Cornelia began to relax. As she did, she spoke more openly about her experiences in London and the loss of her parents.

It was a wound that had scarred her deeply, and the emotions of her father's death were still raw and unforgiving. She was disposed to bouts of tearfulness, and Madeline would sit and comfort her as she wept. How Wesley Stoddard could have neglected her in such a manner was quite beyond Madeline's comprehension, and she assured Cornelia that she had no intention of sending her away.

"Do you promise?" Cornelia asked. As the two took tea together three days after the young girl's arrival.

"I do, and I shall certainly not allow you to be sent to some terrible boarding school. I myself am lucky to have always had my aunt. Even when my parents died, I knew I had her, but you have no one. Except now you do, for I promise that I shall not allow that man to treat you in such a terrible manner," Madeline replied, passing Cornelia a plate of cakes.

"I hated it at Puthall House. It is so dark and foreboding, there are shadows everywhere and strange noises," Cornelia replied, shuddering.

"Puthall Abbey has its share of ghosts. If you ask Mrs. Morrison, she will swear that she saw the figure of one of the sisters who lived here when it was a convent. She was walking along the picture gallery, dressed all in black. It is there that the nuns used to walk on their way to the refectory," Madeline replied, smiling at Cornelia, who looked at her with wide eyes.

"A ghost?" she said, looking about her and jumping as the door opened and Mrs. Morrison herself came bustling in.

"It is just a story, do not worry."

"I am sorry to disturb you, ma'am, but I have a calling card. I will tell the gentleman to go away, though, if you wish. It would be my pleasure to do so," the housekeeper said, presenting Madeline with the card upon a silver tray, an angry look upon her face.

"Oh, and I thought we had heard the last of him," Madeline said, looking down at the card.

It belonged to Lord Stoddard. Mrs. Morrison repeated the fact that he was waiting in the hallway. Cornelia looked scared, and she clutched at Madeline as though a host of Wesley's were about to swoop upon her and carry her off to boarding school there and then.

"You must not worry, Cornelia. Go and sit over there. We shall receive Lord Stoddard and make our position clear," Madeline said, sitting up straight and nodding to Mrs. Morrison, who tutted and left the room.

A few moments later, she returned and announced Lord Wesley Stoddard to the room. He was dressed in riding clothes and looked nervous as he entered.

Bowing slightly to Madeline, he cast a glance at Cornelia, who turned away from him.

"Miss Crenshaw, I..." Wesley began.

"If you have come here to demand Cornelia's return, then you may leave immediately," Madeline replied, cutting him off in mid-sentence.

"I maintain that it is to me and not to you that her father entrusted her," Wesley replied. "Milton and I were good friends, I owe him much, even though the reading of his will came as something of a surprise to me

"If you insist upon dooming Cornelia to the harsh regime of a boarding school then I shall fight you with all I have. She needs proper care and attention after the shock of losing her father under such tragic circumstances. She has no desire to return to live with you at Puthall House, I can tell you this with certainty," Madeline said. Glancing at Cornelia, who nodded.

"Then, you will be pleased that I am willing to reconsider my position upon the matter if I am convinced that Cornelia is well cared for here," Wesley said.

Madeline was taken aback by his words. She had expected him to demand the return of his ward and perhaps even to threaten force if she were not handed over immediately. She knew that her position was tenuous, for the will had clearly stated that Wesley was Cornelia's legal guardian. Until she came of age, by which time she could have spent many miserable years in a boarding school, rather than in the company of someone who cared for her.

"I see," Madeline replied, eyeing Wesley with suspicion.

"The last few days have allowed me to rethink my position. I was a fool, a heartless one at that, to treat Cornelia in such a way. But I must admit that children are a mystery to me. I had such an awful childhood myself that I find reminders of it somewhat difficult. I was brought up a certain way and believed that was how children should be treated. Cornelia's presence has been just such a reminder of that. I believe I acted as my father acted without thinking of how that made me feel. I may reconsider the girl's situation... but I must know she is being well cared for, that is my duty, and I must live up to it," he replied, sighing and shaking his head.

Madeline nodded and was willing to give him the benefit of her doubts. His tone had changed, and there was something of a sense of remorse in his voice. Though it seemed the idea of a boarding school remained at the back of his mind.

"Cornelia is happy here. We have spent many pleasant hours together over the past few days, and I will not see her sent away. However, you are her legal guardian, and I understand that you take your responsibility to her father seriously. That you wish to see that she is well cared for. It is an entirely reasonable proposal," Madeline replied.

"I am glad we agree upon something, Miss Crenshaw," he replied.

"Perhaps then, you would like to spend Christmas here with us? It will be my first at Puthall Abbey in many years, and I intend for it to be a happy occasion for us all. You will see that Cornelia is well cared for and that I am looking after her to the best of my ability, and you may even enjoy yourself," Madeline said, surprised at her change in attitude towards the lord whom she had so disliked beforehand.

"I ... yes, I should be pleased to do so. Christmas can

be a lonely time when one is on one's own. I should be glad of the company," Wesley replied, offering her a weak smile.

"Would you like that too, Cornelia?" Madeline asked, turning to the little girl who looked at them both with wide eyes.

"So long as he does not send me away," she said as Mrs. Morrison entered the room.

"No one will send you away, my dear," Madeline replied, smiling at her.

"Come now, Cornelia. We must get you ready for bed, it is getting late," Mrs. Morrison said, scowling at Wesley, who blushed.

The housekeeper ushered Cornelia from the room, and Madeline and Wesley were left alone. The anger of the other day was gone, replaced by something of a mutual suspicion. Though Madeline had to admit she was surprised by his change of attitude, at least on the surface.

"As you can see, Cornelia is perfectly happy here with me... she is being well cared for. I am sure her father would prefer that to the... well, the alternative," Madeline said.

"The alternative is not as dire as you might think. I merely required some time to adjust to the presence of a child about the house. That is not so unreasonable, is it?" he asked.

"Perhaps not, though I warn you, Lord Stoddard, I shall have no tricks played on me. Cornelia is not going to a boarding school unless she herself expresses a desire to do so," Madeline replied, fixing him with a hard stare.

"I have no intention of doing so, Miss Crenshaw. All I wish is to see Cornelia flourish where I have failed. You clearly know far more about raising a child than I do. For that I am willing to submit to your recommendations on the matter, though I still believe that a robust education would do her good," he replied.

"Of course, but boarding schools are for boys. A girl like Cornelia would find herself in the hands of a finishing school, forced to recount French verbs and learn the rudiments of painting. Having spent just a few days with her, I can assure you that there is far more to Cornelia than that. She is a delightful girl, and I intend to do everything I can to help her flourish," Madeline replied.

Lord Stoddard nodded and prepared to take his leave. It was clear to Madeline that something in him had thawed and that his heart had grown softer towards the girl who had been placed in his charge. She felt some sympathy for him. After all, one could hardly expect a man to so naturally take on the role of a parent. Especially if his own understanding of parenthood was not a good one. Perhaps he really did feel out of his depth and felt that the only solution to his predicament would be to find a school where they were used to dealing with the emotions of young ladies. It was not unreasonable, she thought to herself.

"I shall wish you a good evening then, Miss Crenshaw. I thank you again for the invitation to spend Christmas with you. It really is most kind, and as long as Cornelia is happy for me to do so, I shall look forward to joining you to celebrate the season," he said, bowing to her.

"Will you be attending church, Lord Stoddard? I hear the bells are not to your liking," Madeline said, and he blushed again as she smiled at him before he left the room.

It seemed that some of the ice had thawed, and the brazenness of his disposition had melted away. He had been almost amicable, and when she informed Mrs. Morrison a little later that Lord Stoddard would be joining them for Christmas, the housekeeper could not help but express her surprise.

"Him, ma'am? Why ever have you invited *him*?" she asked, tutting loudly.

"He is Cornelia's legal guardian, but I assure you that he will only be permitted to remain if all talk of boarding schools is renounced. He has at least agreed that Cornelia may remain here with us and admitted that he has felt somewhat out of his depth," Madeline said.

"Well, ma'am, you will forgive me if I still think of him as Lord Muck, until he proves himself otherwise, that is," Mrs. Morrison replied.

"Come now, Agatha. It is Christmas after all," Madeline said, smiling at the housekeeper who just shook her head and walked off.

But Madeline was determined to make this work. She had no desire to be on permanently bad terms with her neighbor, despite her anger at him over Cornelia and the lawn. Perhaps there was more to Wesley Stoddard than she had first imagined. If one could not see something of the good in another at Christmas time, then when could one?

"It will be all right," Madeline assured Cornelia, as Christmas approached.

"And he has promised not to send me away?" Cornelia replied.

"I will not let him. I will not let him do anything that you do not agree to, and if he attempts to send you away, then I will be the first to come after you," Madeline replied, certain that she was more than a match for Lord Stoddard. Whatever he might try.

CHAPTER EIGHT

*M*adeline had always loved Christmas. She remembered the childhood celebrations she had spent at Puthall Abbey fondly. Her aunt too, had always delighted in the season, and the house was always lavishly decorated. As Christmas Eve arrived, she instructed the servants to ensure that the house was decked in all the finery they could muster.

A tree was cut in Bluebell Woods and erected in the hall. It was covered in hundreds of decorations, and a sea of candles was all twinkling as the evening approached. She and Cornelia had spent much of the day preparing paper chains and hanging holly and ivy on every conceivable object so that the house could not have looked more festive and welcoming if the Regent himself were to have been coming for dinner.

Madeline had invited Alice Davies to join them, and so they would be a party of four to begin the celebrations and dine together that evening. She had bought Cornelia a pretty blue dress, and the young girl had come alive as Christmas approached though she had confessed on more than one occasion that she missed her father dearly.

"He is looking down upon us, as is my Aunt Vicky. They would both want us to enjoy a happy Christmas together, I assure you of that," Madeline told her, as they waited for their guests to arrive.

There were presents stacked beneath the decorated tree, and the paper chains had been hung across the hallways. The whole of the abbey appeared bedecked for the celebrations, and Madeline smiled at her efforts, which she knew her aunt would have approved of. A wonderful smell of roasting goose and steaming puddings wafted from the kitchens and outside, a flurry of snow had fallen, making the gardens appear ever so attractive.

"It is all so beautiful," Cornelia said, looking around her.

"I am glad you like it. I just hope our guests do too," Madeline replied, embracing Cornelia, who sighed.

"Do ... do you think he will come?" she asked Madeline.

"He will, I am sure. But there is nothing to worry about. Do not forget that your dear father thought highly of him. At Christmas, we must always make an extra special effort to be kind to those whom we may prefer not to be," Madeline said just as a knock came at the door.

Their first guest was Alice Davies, her shawl and bonnet covered in snow and a bundle of gifts under her arms.

"My, my, how beautiful, Madeline," Alice said, looking around her.

"I think my aunt would approve," Madeline replied, helping her friend with her shawl.

"I am certain she would. Hello, Cornelia, dear, and you look pretty as a picture in your dress," Alice said, kissing Cornelia on the cheek.

A few moments later, there came another knock at the door. Mrs. Morrison opened it, standing back to reveal Lord Stoddard equally as covered in snow as Alice had been. He took off his hat and brushed down his shoulders and stomped his feet on the step as he crossed the threshold.

"Lord Stoddard, ma'am," the housekeeper said, eyeing Wesley with disdain.

"Yes, thank you, Agatha. Good evening, Lord Stoddard, I am pleased you could join us," Madeline said, as she and Cornelia stepped forward.

He was looking around him in amazement at the decorations. He smiled at them both. A smile which neither of them had seen before and which Madeline returned, as Mrs. Morrison took his coat and hat.

"I am pleased I was invited, and I am astounded by the decorations, it is like nothing I have ever seen before. Hello, Cornelia. You look very nice in your new dress, did Madeline buy it for you?" he asked.

Cornelia nodded, standing close to Madeline, who put her hand on her shoulder.

"My aunt had picked up some of the traditions of the

continent on her travels as a young girl with her father. Puthall Abbey has always been lavishly decorated at Christmas time. I have many happy memories from my childhood of the festivities here. I wanted Cornelia to see it too," Madeline replied.

"How splendid, and what wonderful aromas are coming from the kitchen. It seems as though we are to have a feast," Wesley said, smiling again.

"A goose and a pudding. I helped to make the pies," Cornelia said, startling Wesley as she spoke up.

"Did you now? Well ... well, that is excellent. Well done, you," Wesley replied, as Madeline ushered them all into the drawing room for drinks before dinner.

That room, just like all the others, had been lavishly decorated. Cornelia had assisted Madeline in covering every picture and ornament in trails of paper decorations and mistletoe. Wesley looked around him in awe, as Madeline handed him a glass of sherry and bid him sit with them near to the roaring fire.

"I have always loved this room at Christmas time. It feels so snug. Your aunt and I used to sit here in the winter and sew and take tea," Alice said, settling herself next to Cornelia.

"What was Christmas like for you as a child, Lord Stoddard?" Madeline asked, looking at Wesley, who was still looking around him in awe.

"I ... oh, quite different to this," he replied, shaking his head and making no further response.

Madeline had imagined his own childhood to have been like hers. The privilege of rank and class offering any number of delightful experiences and memories to draw upon. It seemed strange that he found all that was so familiar to her to be delightfully new. Again, he commented upon the aromas of food and the decorations around him. It was as though something new had been ignited within him, and he was delighting in every moment of the evening. He had made a considerable effort in his appearance and was wearing a fine tunic and breeches, his shoes were well-polished, and a handsome cravat hung about his neck. In this more relaxed and genteel state he was handsome, and despite herself Madeline could not help but think so.

A short while later, dinner was announced, and the

party made their way through to the dining room in which Madeline had instructed a vast number of candles to be lit so as to illuminate the fine ceiling above.

"This used to be the chapel when the abbey was a convent," Madeline said, as Wesley commented upon the grandeur of the setting.

"They say there is a ghost that walks here," Alice said, turning to Cornelia, who shrunk back.

"Do not worry, Cornelia. There is no such thing," Wesley said, patting her on the shoulder and she turned to him and smiled.

Madeline could not help but notice his attitude towards his young ward softening, and as they sat down to dinner, a congenial atmosphere reigned. The aromas from the kitchen did justice to the taste, and there issued forth an astonishing array of delicious fare for their consumption. The centerpiece was a goose that could easily have fed twice as many as were around the table. Dishes of vegetables abounded, alongside stuffing's, a boiled ham, and no less than four different sauces. It was a magnificent feast. When the Christmas pudding was set alight the four of them exclaimed in delight at the sight.

"I have never eaten so well in all my life," Wesley said, shaking his head, as a bowl of the pudding was placed before him.

"My aunt was fond of her food, she always insisted upon the best. It is a tradition which I myself have vowed to maintain," Madeline replied.

"And you have maintained it well, my dear Madeline," Alice said, patting her arm.

As the meal concluded, Wesley sat back with a satisfied look upon his face and nodded to Madeline.

"I am grateful to you for your invitation, and I am pleased to see how well Cornelia is being cared for. If this is the standard of her dining, then I can be under no illusions that she has been well looked after," he said, laughing.

"Shall we retire now, and perhaps Alice will play the spinet for us? It is only gathering dust in the drawing room, for I do not play, and it seems such a shame not to hear it. It would remind me of my aunt," Madeline said.

"A splendid idea, if Miss Davies agrees?" Lord Stoddard said, and Alice nodded.

"Certainly, I shall play, so long as the noise is not too much for you, Lord Stoddard," and she winked at him.

"I am sure I shall enjoy it," he replied, and the party made their way to the drawing room where coffee was served. Alice seated herself at the spinet and began to play.

She had an excellent repertoire, the room was soon filled with the sound of a waltz. The instrument was only slightly out of tune, and they tapped their feet along to the music, as Lord Stoddard helped himself to brandy.

"It goes well with coffee, do you not think?" he asked, raising his glass to them.

"Then whilst you drink your brandy, we ladies shall dance," Madeline said, taking Cornelia's hand and leading her into the center of the room.

Alice picked up the pace of the waltz, and soon they were dancing a merry dance around the place. Cornelia spun Madeline this way and that, and eventually, they both collapsed in a heap of laughter as the music came to an end.

"Goodness me, I am quite breathless," Madeline exclaimed, laughing and clutching her side.

"Are you saying that the dancing is at an end? I have not yet had the honor," Wesley said, laying aside his glass and stepping forward.

Madeline nodded and smiled; it would do no harm to dance with Wesley. It was Christmas, after all. She turned to Alice, who raised her eyebrows and gave her a pointed look, but once more, she began to play, and another merry waltz was struck up. Wesley took Madeline in his arms and they began to dance, whilst Cornelia stood to one side, clapping along to the music.

They twirled and whirled about the room, each moving effortlessly with the other and discovering that each was as good a dancer as the other. Madeline could not remember the last time she had so enjoyed dancing with a man, and as the waltz came to an end, she urged Alice to play again, her earlier fatigue quite forgotten.

"You dance very well indeed, Miss Crenshaw,"

Wesley said, as she performed a particularly tricky move with all the dexterity of a professional.

"My Aunt Vicky taught me to dance as a child, right here in this drawing room. She would sit at the spinet and play all manner of wonderful tunes, and I would dance, sometimes with my father and sometimes with my mother. Mrs. Morrison has even been known to dance at times," Madeline said, laughing as he spun her around.

Turning, she spun into him, and their eyes met, long enough for their lips to almost come together. An act which caused Wesley to blush and turn away.

"Forgive me," he said, laughing and looking at her shyly.

"The dance, we have not finished the dance," she said, taking hold of his hands and spinning him around, not minding in the least what had almost just passed.

A few moments later, he bowed out and took a stiff drink of his brandy, as Madeline came to sit by Cornelia. Wesley was gathering up his things and preparing to leave.

"Are you going so soon, Lord Stoddard? The night is still young, and I am sure Alice will continue to play for us," Madeline said, a little confused by his swift departure.

"No, no. I must be going and apologize to you for the suggestion that Cornelia would be unhappy in your care. I can see that she is entirely happy. I thank you again for your hospitality this evening. It really has been a delight," he said, as Madeline nodded and wished him a good night.

"You do not have to leave so suddenly, Lord Stoddard. Why not stay a little while, we intend to play all manner of party games," she said, catching his arm.

"No, no, thank you, I must be going," he said and calling for his coat and hat he made his way out onto the terrace and across the lawn.

Madeline watched him go with a confused look. It seemed that she and Wesley were just beginning to know one another better. Was it his embarrassment that they had nearly kissed that had caused him to run away? It was Christmas, and one would expect such things beneath the mistletoe. She hardly considered it an impropriety though she remained quite astonished at the change which had come over him. Clearly, he no longer considered her a threat, nor believed that Cornelia was better off anywhere but at Puthall Abbey. As she watched him disappear into the darkness of the Christmas night, Cornelia came to stand next to her and slipped her hand into hers.

"I wish he had been like that always," she whispered.

"So do I, Cornelia, dear, so do I," Madeline replied.

Wesley hurried through the snow, which had fallen thickly since his arrival at the abbey earlier that evening. Twice he stumbled, as he made his way home and cursed himself as he floundered in the drifts. But it was as much his foolishness that evening that he was lamenting as it was the inclement weather.

What a fool he had been in so many ways. In the past days, he had come to recognize just how cruel his actions towards Cornelia had been. He had thought back a great deal to his own childhood and lamented the treatment he had received at the hand of his father. His own attitude towards Cornelia was born of his past, yet it was no excuse to treat the young girl in such a manner. Thanks to Madeline, he had come to see this. But it was not just his treatment of Cornelia that caused him to curse himself. It was the kiss he had almost planted upon Madeline's lips. How foolish he was, he should have been kinder to them all, and perhaps then the feelings which that moment had aroused in him might have been realized.

Since their interview at Puthall Abbey on the day she had invited him to dine on Christmas Eve, Wesley had found himself dwelling upon Madeline. She was extremely pretty, but it was not just her looks which attracted him. She had a fiery spirit within her and a temperament which spoke of determination in the face of any situation. She was intelligent and witty, not to mention kind and considerate. Qualities that he found immensely attractive, and this had caused his temporary loss of composure as he had leaned in for the kiss.

As he arrived at Puthall House, Brooks and the other servants had just wished one another a happy

Christmas and exchanged their Christmas gifts. The valet looked at his master in surprise, for they had not expected him to return so early from the abbey.

"My Lord? Is everything all right?" the valet asked, and Wesley nodded but made no reply, shaking his head and going to his study.

For once, there was a fire kindled in the grate, and he poured himself a brandy, slumping into an armchair and lamenting his lot. Cornelia was clearly better off with Madeline, that much was certain. It was too late now to mend the errors of the past. All he could hope was that neither of them bore a grudge against him or made it known how abysmally he had treated them.

He was about to pour another drink when there came a knock at the door.

"Go to bed, Brooks. It is Christmas, you should have your leisure and rest," he replied.

But the door opened, and instead of the valet, it was Madeline who stood in the doorway, a smile upon her face.

CHAPTER NINE

"*I* trust I am not disturbing you, Lord Stoddard," she said, closing the door behind her and standing before him.

She had followed him almost immediately, leaving Cornelia in the care of Alice at the abbey. She was unsure why. After all, only a short while ago, she had been somewhat nervous as to his company that evening. Yet now, here she was, standing in his study, uncertain why she had come. She wanted to thank him for his change of heart, though why she needed to do so was quite beyond her. Something had drawn her to him, and she tilted her head to one side, waiting for his reply.

"I... no, what else does one do on Christmas Eve than ... well, this?" he said, pointing to the brandy glass.

"You could have had another brandy at the abbey. I... I just wanted to thank you for your kindness to us all. I had expected... well, I had expected something else. Given our previous encounters," she replied.

"Our previous encounters were hardly fruitful, and I must admit to having been just a little scared of you," he admitted, taking a drink of brandy and offering her the armchair opposite him.

Madeline smiled, she had never considered herself to be scary to anyone, least of all a member of the aristocracy. It seemed strange to think that he had been intimidated by her when she herself had found him a challenging opponent to spar with.

"I am sorry you took off so suddenly. We could have played charades or blind man's bluff. Cornelia would have loved that, and it seemed as though you were enjoying yourself in her company," Madeline said.

"I... I was, but you see the problem I have, is that I am unable to truly enjoy myself for I have never done so," he said, a note of sadness creeping into his voice.

"What do you mean?" she asked, looking at him in puzzlement.

"I never enjoyed Christmas as a child. My mother would take to her bed, and my father would remind me that children should be seen and not heard, and even then, he wished to see as little of me as possible. I never received a present or saw a decoration. He believed such things to be frivolities. I was told to read a book on Christmas Day rather than sit down to a lavish meal and play party games," he said, sighing sadly.

How awful, Madeline thought to herself, though perhaps it explained something of his treatment towards Cornelia. If he had never experienced a childhood of his own, then how could he possibly give a childhood to another?

"But you need not use your own father as your pattern," she said, smiling at him.

"But I did, at least at first and the poor girl must have been in such a state. It is no wonder that she ran away from me," Wesley said with a mournful expression upon his face.

"But surely you have changed? You have realized the

error of your ways now, and you are a better person for it. I can see it in you, Wesley. I saw it this evening," she replied.

"I was uncertain what I might find at Puthall Abbey and whether Cornelia would be treated as you suggested she would be. I knew my own failings, but I could not see her passed around to others who would neglect her as equally as I did at first. Tonight, I saw a child who was happy. And given the tragedy of recent events that is quite remarkable. It showed me that my own father's behavior towards me was wrong and that a child should be given the love and care she deserves to thrive. Not sent to the corner or reduced to being seen and not heard. I saw a different way of life, Madeline ... Miss Crenshaw," he said, blushing at his faux pas.

Madeline paused for a moment, and then, quite instinctively, she reached out and took his hand in hers, smiling as she did so. He looked up nervously, the tremor of a smile playing upon his own lips. For a moment, she saw that little boy, so browbeaten by his father into submission and so scared of being chastised simply for enjoying the delights of childhood.

"You are quite different from the man I encountered some weeks ago. The one upon my lawns," she said, and he nodded.

"I... I have a lot to learn, but there is the chance to learn it, perhaps..." he said as he traced the line of her fingers with his.

"I must say that when you asked me to dance, I was somewhat surprised, though I should very much like to do so again," she said, and he blushed an even deeper shade of red.

"I... I would like that too, Miss Crenshaw," he said.

"Madeline, please, and perhaps I will call you Wesley. Though I know your title goes back to pre-reformation times," she said, laughing as he shook his head.

"I can be a pompous old thing at times, but you and Cornelia are better off without me. I am so set in my ways, I would hardly be the companion which either of you deserves. Cornelia deserves someone who will show her the things I do not understand and you..." he said, his words trailing off.

"I need a man of my own choosing, one who can

change his ways for the better as you have done. As for Cornelia, I would say you have already realized the error of your previous ways and set about making amends," she said, rising from her chair.

"Perhaps," he replied.

She stepped forward and knelt quickly, placing a chaste kiss upon his cheek and smiling at him, and as he raised his hand to his face in some disbelief, she bid him goodnight.

"I must get back to Cornelia now, it is getting late. I would not wish to be stuck in a snowdrift. Goodnight, Wesley, and I would be delighted if you would join us tomorrow to continue the celebrations," she said, and with that, she was gone.

Outside, she breathed a sigh of relief. Her encounter with Wesley had gone far better than she had envisioned. She was surprised at herself for the boldness of planting a kiss upon his cheek. Still, she felt no sense of regret. The moon had appeared from behind a cloud, and the snow had stopped falling. The landscape was still, that silent and holy night, lying crisp and even. She set off across the meadow, the crunch of the snow beneath her feet and a chill in the air.

"Goodnight, Wesley," she said, turning back towards Puthall House as she reached the abbey, "and thank you."

CHAPTER TEN

Christmas morning dawned brightly, though a fresh fall of snow had occurred overnight. The bells of the church sounded across the village as Madeline and Cornelia returned from the morning service.

Once back, the little girl sat with Mrs. Morrison in the drawing room.

"Come with me," Alice whispered to Madeline. "I have something for her."

The two women left.

Cornelia was happily engaged with Mrs. Morrison.

Together they read a book and ate cookies. The child sprang up in delight as Madeline and Alice entered.

"Hello, Cornelia, my dear, and a happy Christmas once again," Alice said, embracing her and handing her the large box which between them she and Madeline had carried from the village.

"Goodness, what is it?" Cornelia asked, pulling off the large bow and tentatively removing the lid.

She let out a gasp of delight and held up an exquisite gown, decorated with the finest sequins and lace. It was a sky blue. She rushed upstairs to try it on immediately, followed by Mrs. Morrison who passed comment upon "not spoiling the child" but also admitted that the dress was very beautiful.

"You are very kind, Alice," Madeline said, smiling at her friend.

"Well, Cornelia reminds me so very much of you when you were a child. Do you remember the dress I bought you when you were around Cornelia's age? The one with the green sash, you looked a picture in it," Alice said.

"I do remember it, of course, I do. I wore it at every

party I was taken to, so they started calling me "the little green girl" because I wore it so much," Madeline said, laughing.

A few moments later, Cornelia returned, and she looked as pretty as Madeline had imagined her to be. A real lady and far beyond her age.

"It fits perfectly, ma'am," the housekeeper said, looking proudly down at Cornelia, who twirled the dress about her.

"Oh, I am so pleased," Alice said, beaming at the delighted child.

Madeline smiled. She was so pleased to see Cornelia happy after all the difficulties of the past months. Like Madeline herself, she knew that the young girl would never forget her parents but perhaps together they could be a family and find peace and happiness. Cornelia was already a delightful little girl, Madeline had no doubt that she would grow into an even finer young woman.

"Now, Cornelia, do you have something for Alice?" Madeline asked, and Cornelia nodded and went to the bureau.

From inside, she drew out not one but two little boxes, and she returned to stand before them smiling.

"I made one for you both," she said, holding out the boxes to Madeline and Alice.

Both women looked in delight and surprise at the gifts. Madeline had known of Alice's intended kindness, and she had encouraged the young girl to make a present for her friend, but she had not realized that Cornelia would do the same for her. Inside the boxes were the most delightful little necklaces, made from little stones she had found in the garden. They were crude, of course, but the thought behind them was sincere and from the heart.

"They are lovely, Cornelia," Madeline said, and both women put them on at once and admired each other as they did so.

"I shall wear it to the next Church Guild meeting," Alice said, "and I shall tell everyone that it came from the abbey."

"There's nothing here for Wesley, though. He seemed so much nicer last night at the dinner, and I so enjoyed seeing you both dance," Cornelia said, sounding sad and forlorn as she did so.

Madeline smiled and took her hand.

"It is all right, Cornelia. I am sure Wesley has plenty of presents, but it is kind of you to think of him. You certainly have a good heart. I think you will grow up to be a very generous and loving person," she said, patting her on the shoulder.

Cornelia's words rang true with her, though she kept her thoughts private. She also wished she had something to give to Wesley. Some token of affection or sign of thanks. Madeline had come to see him in an entirely different light, and she secretly wished that he had offered to escort her home. As she had walked across the snowy meadow the night before, her mind had wandered to the possibility of a kiss, shared beneath the moonlight. But perhaps that was all idle fancy, she could hardly expect that radical a change in him. It amazed her that her own feelings could be so altered, given that in the past she had been so set against the idea of a husband. Her first encounter with Wesley had only confirmed that notion further. But in the past few days she had come to see the man in an entirely different light.

What he had suffered as a child had been terrible, and he was striving to overcome it.

As Cornelia and Alice chatted about her dress and all the lovely things which Christmas would bring, Madeline looked up at her aunt's portrait on the wall and smiled. Vicky loved Christmas, and she would have loved the company of Cornelia too. Madeline imagined her and the child causing mischief and playing pranks on the servants. That was always what she and her aunt did at Christmas time. They had once hidden all the teaspoons from Mrs. Morrison and sent her on a merry chase about the house before finally revealing their deception.

She was so grateful to her aunt. Not only for all the happy memories of her childhood but also for leaving Puthall Abbey to her so that she might continue that legacy. Madeline was determined to make it a place of joy and happiness for Cornelia. A place where she would feel safe and secure and where she could grow up surrounded by love. She smiled to herself and whispered a thank you to her aunt's portrait, which looked down with its smiling face upon her. It reminded her that whilst Puthall Abbey stood, her aunt's spirit was very much alive.

"Now then, what say we have some fun before we sit down to luncheon? I think we have time for a few games before Mrs. Morrison calls us in," Madeline said, and Cornelia clapped her hands together in delight.

But just as she did so, there came a commotion outside and the sound of raised voices coming from the hallway.

"Sir, Your Lordship, you cannot just burst in here like this," Mrs. Morrison could be heard shouting.

"Mrs. Morrison, my dear, it is Christmas Day, a season of peace and goodwill amongst all men. I have brought gifts. A gift for you and for all," came the sound of Wesley's voice.

"Goodness, whatever is happening?" Alice asked as the three of them turned towards the door, beyond which came the exciting sounds.

A moment later it flew open, and Wesley was standing there with Brooks at his side. Each of them was bearing all manner of boxes and parcels tied up with ribbons.

"Ma'am, His Lordship is here to see you," Mrs.

Morrison said, quite breathless with excitement, "and it seems he has brought us all some good cheer."

Wesley was smiling broadly, and he put down his boxes and held out his arms.

"A Merry Christmas to you, a happy feast, and may God bless us all on this happy day," he said.

Madeline looked at him in delighted disbelief. She could hardly believe the transformation, and it was as though the true spirit of Christmas had entered his heart and caused an overflowing of joy within him.

"A Merry Christmas to you, too," she replied. "Will you join us?"

CHAPTER ELEVEN

*W*esley stepped forward, taking off his snow-covered hat and scarf and seating himself on the floor next to Cornelia, who smiled at him. There appeared no fear in her now, and she took his hand in hers and looked at him with all the innocence of childhood. Which is so often far more trusting and willing to forgive than any grown person could ever be.

"Happy Christmas, Wesley, do you like my new dress? It is a gift from Alice," she said.

He smiled at her and nodded.

"I like it very much, and I have a present for you too,

Cornelia," he said, signaling to Brooks, who stepped forward with a large box tied up with a pretty pink bow.

"Goodness, you will spoil the child, My Lord," Mrs. Morrison said, as Cornelia began to undo the bow about the box.

"You must open your gift as well, my dear Mrs. Morrison. Tis' the season for generosity after all," Wesley said, as the housekeeper opened her own small box and gasped.

"Why, sir, I have never seen such generosity," she said, blushing.

"And there is much more to come," Wesley replied, turning back to Cornelia, who had just opened the box.

Madeline looked over her shoulder and could not believe the sight which greeted her. There, lying amidst exquisite tissue paper, was a doll. But it was not just any doll, it was perhaps the finest doll which Madeline had ever seen. It was dressed in a pretty pink gown and came with a hat and other accessories. The hair and face were so lifelike that it was almost as though another child had walked into the room.

Cornelia took it from the box with an expression of great delight upon her face. She turned to Wesley and beamed and clasped the doll to her in an embrace.

"What a beautiful doll, Wesley," Madeline exclaimed.

"I love her," Cornelia said.

"And what will you call her?" Alice asked, kneeling beside Cornelia, who held the doll out to her.

"Perhaps ... I shall call her Victoria, or Vicky for short," Cornelia replied, and they all agreed that that was an excellent idea.

"Cornelia, there is another gift I wish to give you. Though it is not wrapped up in a box with a bow. It is an apology. You are still young, but you have seen and experienced things well beyond your years. When you arrived at Puthall House... I should have done far more to make you welcome. Instead, I was heartless and aloof. I did not mean to be, but you see,

I had a most unhappy childhood, and I dreaded the thought that you would experience such a thing at my hands too. So, instead of welcoming you, I made things worse."

He stopped and looked down. Cornelia hugged her doll and smiled.

"Your father was a good friend to me, and it is an honor that he has entrusted you to my care. But I am no parent. In the past few days, I have seen how happy you are here at Puthall Abbey with Madeline. I promise, and this is my further gift, that I will do everything I can to make you happy and to see you flourish in your new surroundings. You are a delightful girl, and you have taught me a great deal. I promise there will be no more talk of sending you away, and I will certainly not be distant from you. I can no longer be haunted by the ghosts of the past. I must look to the future instead. A future, I hope, which includes you," Wesley said, smiling at Cornelia, who put down the doll and threw her arms around him.

At first, Wesley seemed at a loss as to what to do. His eyes went instinctively to Madeline, who gestured to him. With a slight hesitation, he placed his arms around Cornelia, and the two embraced. The anguish of the past weeks replaced by a mutual understanding of what it is to suffer loss but to discover a happier future.

"Does this mean I can stay with Madeline?" Cornelia asked, her hands still upon his shoulders.

"Well, I think Madeline makes an ideal companion for you and you for her. But we must ask Madeline first before we impose further upon her hospitality. What do you not think?" Wesley asked, and they both looked up at Madeline, who smiled.

"Cornelia may stay at Puthall Abbey for just as long as she wishes for we have become the best of friends, have we not?" Madeline said, and Cornelia nodded and beamed.

She took up her doll and went to show her to Mrs. Morrison, who was still in a state of shock following Lord Stoddard's generous gift. Brooks too had received the largest Christmas gift which his employer had ever given him. With a glass of sherry in hand, he was happily sat watching proceedings from the side of the room. Alice had taken to the spinet, and she was playing all manner of delightful tunes so that the room was filled with such happiness. Just as it had been when Aunt Vicky was its custodian, her portrait smiled down at them from above the mantelpiece.

Madeline smiled at Wesley, and he nodded to her. The two of them stepped out onto the terrace where the morning had turned bright and chilly. Their breath frosted in the air, and the lawns were covered in a thick layer of snow. It gave the look of an artist's Christmas scene.

"Thank you for your kindness to Cornelia," Madeline said, as they stood together on the terrace.

"It is no kindness. It is what the child deserves, a happy home. She will be far better off here at the abbey with you than at Puthall House with me. I am no parent, whilst I shall endeavor to treat her with all the love and care she deserves, there will still be times when I need reminding of my parental duties," he said, laughing.

"Cornelia may stay here for as long as she wishes, and we shall see to it that she receives a proper education. For a start, I am sure she would delight in learning the spinet from Alice, and the library here is filled with books. Between us, we shall give her a first-rate education," Madeline said.

"Let it be so," he replied, and from his pocket, he took out a small box, neatly tied with a bow and which he now presented to her. "A present and a token of my thanks for all you have done for me."

"I have done nothing," she replied, blushing as she took the gift and began to unwrap it.

"On the contrary, you have done more than you know. You have reminded me of what it is to be a human being and not some emotionless creature too afraid of his past to confront it. You and Cornelia have shown me that, and I will forever be grateful to you," he said, watching as she opened the box.

Inside was an exquisite diamond ring, the stone sparkling in the light of that chilly Christmas morning. Madeline gasped at the sight, for she had never seen anything like it before. The jewel sat upon a gold inlay, the band fitted her finger perfectly.

"Wesley, it is beautiful. Thank you," she said, holding the ring up to the light and smiling at him.

"It belonged to my late mother who, though often absent, could be kind too. I wish I had known her better, perhaps my childhood would have been happier had I done so," he said, taking her hand.

"And what of the future? You said you would not let the past imprison you. Do you mean that?" she asked.

"I do, Madeline, I truly do. Though I would ask that you help me in that task... if you would? You are the Christmas gift that has healed my heart. I will be forever thankful to you for that," he said.

"No more riding across my lawn?" she asked, smiling at him.

"No more riding across your lawn, though perhaps I might still make the walk here?" he said, their hands still joined together, as he smiled at her.

"You may walk here as often as you like, whenever you like," she replied. "There is always an open door to you at Puthall Abbey."

"As there is for you at Puthall House," he said, and

he leaned forward and kissed her on the cheek, as the two stood together on the terrace hand in hand.

Back inside, there were more gifts to open and delight in. Wesley had gone quite over the top with his lavish presents. Cornelia and Madeline received all manner of fine things to wear, eat and play with. Alice received sheet music for the spinet and the promise that one would be delivered to her cottage in the New Year.

"Just in time for you to play for us during the long months of winter," Wesley said, as Alice clapped her hands together in delight.

"I have always wanted my own spinet," she said, as she showed Cornelia the basic chords and together they played.

"And it will be the finest spinet I can procure," Wesley said.

"You can procure, My Lord?" Brooks raised his glass to Wesley, who blushed.

"All right then, that you can procure, Brooks. I will

send you up to town to shop for me," Wesley replied, smiling at his valet who nodded.

Very soon, they were called into lunch, and as had always been the tradition at Puthall Abbey, the servants joined them in the dining room. It was fortunate that the room was large, for there were twenty who sat down to dinner on that happy Christmas Day. Madeline was at the head of the table. Cornelia took it upon herself to help the maids serve before they all sat down to eat.

"I could get used to this," Mrs. Morrison said, settling herself down next to Brooks.

There was all manner of good things to eat. The table was groaning under the weight of the food. Madeline had decided that no expense should be spared for the celebration of Christmas, and despite the need for some economy, now was not the time to pinch the pennies. All the servants received a Christmas box, which Cornelia handed out at the end of the meal. She really was a delightful little girl, and the more that Madeline watched her, the more she reminded her of herself when she was a child.

"Aunt Vicky would have loved this," Madeline said to Mrs. Morrison, as they came to the pudding course.

"She would have done, ma'am. She loved Christmas. I remember her saying once, 'Agatha, I wish it could be Christmas every day and that we could eat, drink and be merry together like this always,' and I said, 'well, ma'am, no work would get done if it were,' but I do not think she was too worried about that. You are ever so like her, ma'am, if you will pardon me saying so," Mrs. Morrison replied.

"I take it as a compliment, Mrs. Morrison. I loved my Aunt Vicky more than anyone else in the world. I miss her so very much." Madeline knew that the sadness was already starting to lift. That soon, there would be more good memories and less grief.

"She will always be watching over you, ma'am. And she would have been so proud of you for taking in the young girl and giving her a home," Mrs. Morrison replied, patting her arm as she turned back to Brooks, who had surreptitiously charged her glass.

On Madeline's other side was Wesley, and with the

pudding now served, he rose from his place and tapped his glass to call for quiet.

"What a happy gathering this is and how blessed we are to be together on this day of celebration. I do not wish to sound somber, but there have often been occasions on which I have not enjoyed Christmas, but I feel that today is the first of many Christmases, which I shall delight in. I have you all to thank for that in welcoming me to Puthall Abbey. There is one person, however, whom I must thank above all, and that is dear Madeline here," he said, raising his glass to her as she blushed.

"There is no need ..." she began, but Wesley held up his hand.

"There is every need. You, Madeline, have shown me what it is to put away the ghost of the past and look to the future. You have made me realize that one cannot live in the past or be held back by its precepts. I propose a toast to you and a toast to the happiness of the future. For us all," he said, raising his glass as those gathered around the table stood and called out the toast.

"To Madeline and future happiness," they said, and

there was much clinking of glasses and passing of bottles.

The lunch went on long into the afternoon, and as twilight drew in, Madeline asked for the oil lamps to be lit, and the fires kindled as they prepared for that other great abbey tradition, the Christmas games. Every Christmas Day, after lunch had been served, her aunt would have the rugs rolled back in the drawing room, and the furniture moved to the side of the room. Candles would be lit all around, and together with the family and the servants, they would play all manner of games.

Madeline was delighted to see the tradition continue. Very soon, there were shouts of laughter and screams coming from the drawing room as together they played blind man's bluff, puss in the corner and hot cockles, a most unusual game involving much guesswork and just a little raucousness. Alice played the spinet as they larked and capered about, and no happier scene could be imagined as that on Christmas afternoon at Puthall Abbey.

After much reveling, Madeline stepped out into the hallway for a moment, and she was joined by Wesley. He was breathless from an energetic game in which he had to carry Cornelia on his shoulders whilst she searched desperately for hanging sweets whilst blindfolded.

"Goodness me, I have never had so much fun," he said, smiling at her as she laughed.

"And I do not think that Cornelia ever has either," Madeline replied, as he mopped his brow.

"She will flourish here with you, I know it," he said.

"And you must promise to be a frequent visitor. I cannot be her sole parent, I shall expect you to play your part," Madeline said, though she had a feeling that keeping Wesley away would not be a problem.

"You shall tire of me, so frequent will my visits be," he said, taking her hand.

"I shall hold you to it," she warned, winking at him.

"What say I show you the intentions of my heart," he said, pointing towards a sprig of mistletoe hanging from the chandelier above.

Madeline blushed, and he offered a chaste kiss upon her cheek. Smiling, together they returned to the celebrations.

If Madeline had been told when she arrived at Puthall Abbey that her heart would be won in such a way, then she would never have believed it. In London, she had had no time for men. They all seemed so arrogant and brazen. She had been courted by all manner of types. They had shared one thing in common, a sense of self-entitlement and a rudeness she had found intolerable. Her first encounter with Wesley Stoddard had only confirmed her prejudices, as had her subsequent encounters with him over Cornelia. She had considered him to be like all the rest and had never, for a moment, thought that there might be a deeper reason for his behavior. But he had revealed himself to be something more, a man who could change. One strong enough to see the errors of his ways. A man with a past who finally confronted it and laid it to rest. No longer would those memories haunt him, of that she was certain. In Wesley Stoddard, she saw the future she had so long denied herself. One she could now embrace.

"Will you both dance with me?" Cornelia asked, as they entered the room to be greeted by the shouts and laughter of the servants still at their party games.

"I think we shall," Wesley replied, taking her hand.

Alice struck up a waltz upon the spinet, and very soon, the whole room was alive with clapping and the stamping of feet. Together they celebrated Christmas with the happiness and style which Aunt Victoria would have wished. All could declare that it was the happiest Christmas any of them had known.

CHAPTER TWELVE

The new spinet arrived in late January. It did much to lift the spirits of all who heard Alice practicing it in her drawing room. Wesley had been as good as his word, it was the very best instrument which money could buy. In fact, he lavished many gifts upon those around him. Eventually, Madeline had to tell him to stop, for she could not possibly wear all of the gowns he had sent from London nor enjoy every one of the fine soaps or talc's which arrived at the abbey on an almost daily basis.

"I am sorry, but I have no one else to spend my money on, except for my friends," he said.

She shook her head and laughed at yet another delightful box arriving from town.

"Your generosity knows no bounds, Wesley," she replied, as the two sat in the drawing room of Puthall Abbey with Cornelia in late January.

The snow had lain on the ground since Christmas, and the fire had been well stoked up against the cold. Mrs. Morrison had just brought in the tea along with a mound of hot buttered teacakes, which Cornelia was already devouring hungrily.

"One would think we never fed the child," Madeline said, laughing, as Cornelia took her third teacake.

"A growing girl needs her food, does she not?" Wesley said, smiling at Cornelia, who nodded.

He had come to dote on the girl, and there was not a day that went by that he did not pay a visit to the abbey to see her and Madeline. They had become closer by the day, and neither had forgotten the kiss they had shared beneath the mistletoe on Christmas Day.

"Are you staying for lunch with us, My Lord?" Mrs. Morrison asked.

"Lunch? We shall hardly need lunch after all these teacakes, Mrs. Morrison. But yes, I should be delighted," he replied.

"Cornelia is going to help in the kitchens today, we are making a Charlotte Russe, and I am sure you shall manage it, along with the teacakes," Mrs. Morrison said.

"How can I say no, Mrs. Morrison?" Wesley replied, rubbing his hands together in delight.

"Come now, Cornelia. The Russe will not make itself, and you have been asking to help cook for some days," Mrs. Morrison said, as Cornelia laid aside her doll and followed the housekeeper from the room.

"She seems already to be growing up. She is truly flourishing," Wesley said, turning to Madeline, who nodded.

"Yes, her French is quite remarkable already. She and I held an entire conversation about the weather the other day over lunch," Madeline replied, "and her drawing skills are far beyond her years."

"She is such a delight," Wesley said, laughing and pointing out of the window at the snow.

"Well, indeed." Madeline lay aside her cup and saucer and smiled.

"Do you know, I have never felt so happy. In all matters, I feel quite at peace. I came to Puthall for some rest and recuperation. I hasten to add that my illness was not of the body but of the mind. I was quite exhausted by life. I thought the countryside might aid my woes, but at first it only added to them. That dark and dingy house, the arrival of Cornelia, and the shock of discovering she was to be my ward. The quiet loneliness of the countryside. It all conspired against me... but then I met you."

He smiled at her, and Madeline felt her heart start to soar.

"You made your presence forcefully known, and everything changed. It would not have mattered where I found myself, the melancholy would have remained had I not met you," he said, taking her hand in his.

"I am glad. Everyone deserves happiness, and you are no exception." The feel of his hand sent warm delight up her arm and into her heart. Maybe she had also received a gift, one of a thaw to her heart in the realms of love. "It is no surprise that you have felt a sense of melancholy over the years. Your childhood was quite abysmal, and the way you were treated leaves me wondering how you ever survived," she replied.

"I barely did. You know, on the day that Cornelia ran away, I was reminded of the day I did just the same. My father had been particularly beastly to me. I had done a drawing of my mother and I was walking in the grounds of our house, and I was so pleased with it that I took it to my father and showed him. I was expecting praise and encouragement but he... he took it from me and tore it in two and threw it in the fire. In his mind, it was nothing but childish fancy and not to be encouraged," he said, a tear in his eye as he spoke.

Madeline could not believe the cruelty of what she was hearing, and she took his other hand in hers and gave him a look of reassurance.

"And so, you ran away?" she asked.

"I did. I went straight back to the nursery and

wrapped a small cake in a handkerchief. It was a seed cake, my nanny used to give me an extra one if I had been good and I had saved it. I went straight back downstairs with the cake in my pocket and snuck out of a side door and set off through the parklands. It was a cold day, I remember, and I had only a thin coat and no hat. I was soon cold and lost. I sat down and began to cry, having eaten the cake whilst I was walking."

"Oh my, you poor thing, what happened?" Madeline squeezed his hand and angled herself so she could look at him.

"It was fortunate that one of my tenant farmers came along and noticed me in the trees. He asked me what I was doing, and I said I was running away. He just laughed and scooped me up and took me home. Well, you can imagine how angry my father was with me. He gave me such a beating that evening that my poor legs were black and blue. I never tried to run away again, but I always dreamed of it. I had heard stories of adventurers on the high seas and explorers in far off lands. How I longed for that to be me and instead, I was trapped in the misery of my father's house," he said sadly.

"And you have carried that burden your whole life. It is no wonder that you thought of coming to the countryside for recuperation. But it is not just me who has helped you, Cornelia has taught you a lot too," she replied, still holding his hands.

"You are right about that," he replied, "she has reminded me that childhood is a precious gift and that even though my own was miserable, that is no reason to cause another's to be so. Cornelia deserves all the happiness that we can give her."

"I am glad you said, 'we' for I have said all along that it must be the both of us who help her. I hope that the two of us might keep up this happy arrangement, for I delight in your company and would not have it any other way than for you to be a frequent visitor," Madeline replied.

In the past month, she had come to look forward to Wesley's company. He was so much a changed man. They had discovered so many shared interests and passions. Each loved to read and dance. They had taken walks together in the snow and visited Alice who had played the spinet for them. Together they had taught Cornelia her lessons and shared stories of their past, much to each other's benefit.

Madeline could not help but feel her emotions towards Wesley deepening, and so it seemed his had for her.

"And I delight in being a frequent visitor, Madeline, but... perhaps there is more," he said, and with a swift movement, he knelt before her, their hands still clasped.

"I..." Madeline said, quite taken by surprise at his actions.

"Madeline, there is only one more thing you could do for me to make me happier than any man in England... that is, agree to be my wife. Marry me, for I have come to love you so very much. I know that with each passing day, I shall fall ever more in love with you. I have never felt such feelings before, and I cannot help but express them now before you," he said, looking up at her with wide and beseeching eyes.

Madeline was astonished by his words, but they delighted her too. She needed no time to think of her response, for it was an emphatic yes.

"I could not think of another man who could have so captured my heart and caused such happiness within me," she replied, placing her arms around him as the two shared a kiss.

"Oh, Madeline, you have made me happier than I have ever been before. What a wonderful life you, Cornelia, and I have ahead of us. The memories of the past are banished, and now we have only the future to look forward to," he said.

She was wearing the ring which he had gifted her at Christmas, and now she took it off her right hand and handed it to him.

"Shall this be our engagement ring?" she asked, as he slid it gently back onto her engagement finger.

"I shall always think of Christmas Day as our anniversary, my darling Madeline. It was then that I realized how in love with you I was. Though the feeling was so new to me that I was uncertain how to react. I wish I had asked you there and then, when we stood out on the terrace together and looked across the lawn. Somehow, it did not seem quite right at that time. Maybe it was a little soon. However, I knew I loved you then, and my love has only grown. Right now, my heart was fit to burst, and I could not bear to wait a moment longer to ask for your hand," he replied, and they kissed. A sweet kiss that took her breath away and let her feel the full force of his love.

"You have my hand, Wesley, and the promise that we shall be together forever. Let us not waste any time, for it is precious, we shall wed just as soon as we can," she replied.

"I agree, and I shall even delight in the sounds of the church bells ringing as they announce our marriage," he replied, laughing as the door opened.

Cornelia was standing there before them, she announced that lunch was now ready, the Charlotte Russe taking center place.

"Cornelia, dear. We have some news to tell you," Madeline said as she and Wesley sat hand in hand.

"I know," Cornelia said, a grin on her face.

"Do you?" Madeline asked.

"You're getting married to Wesley," Cornelia said, causing Madeline to look most surprised.

"Ah, well, that is my doing," Wesley replied, as Cornelia came over and took both their hands. "You see, I thought I had better ask permission before requesting your hand in marriage. It seemed the right thing to do. I am glad to say that Cornelia gave her permission wholeheartedly."

Madeline smiled and embraced them both.

"I am very glad to hear it, and I am sure Aunt Victoria would have given hers too," she said, looking up at the portrait hanging above them.

Aunt Victoria's face almost seemed to have taken on a new radiance. Madeline could hear her delight as if she were present to learn of the engagement. It was certainly not what Madeline had ever imagined, but she had always known her aunt to have her best interests at heart.

"Then everyone is happy it seems," Wesley said, "now then, all this talk of marriage has given me quite an appetite. Will you lead us through to lunch, Cornelia?"

Cornelia nodded, and she took them both by the hand and led them through to the dining room. Together they shared a happy lunch, and it was agreed that Cornelia's Charlotte Russe was the best that any of them had ever tasted.

But there was far more to their happiness than a lavish pudding, for each had now discovered a family. Their loss had been turned to joy. Cornelia once more had parents who would love and care for her. Always honoring the memory of her own dear mother and father whose sense in placing her with Wesley could now be seen. Wesley had found delight in the childhood of another and banished the memories of his own to the past. He could be everything that his own father was not. He would be the very best father he could be. And Madeline had found the happiness which comes when another soul enters one's life. The happiness of companionship and love, both familial and romantic. A love that would last for the rest of her life.

Together they were the happiest of families, and after their marriage Madeline and Wesley lived a long and happy life at Puthall Abbey with Cornelia at their side. They never forgot the past, for it had done so much to shape them. But their eyes were always on the future and that which it would bring.

They grew as a family, and it was often commented upon that no happier family was known in the district. Madeline knew the secret of that happiness all too well. It was very simple, love, and that was all they needed.

"My dear Rosalind, how very nice you look this evening." Wentworth Blackwood, the Duke of Newfield, was as warm and as complimentary as ever.

Rosalind could not help but wonder if he would utter the very same words if she had turned up to the Duke's winter ball in her riding outfit, and an old, worn cloak. She somehow thought he would.

"You flatter me, Your Grace." Rosalind smiled at his pleasant face.

The Duke was portly, with an almost full head of

grey hair and a ruddy complexion. His pale blue eyes shone under the light of the chandeliers and they looked upon her in a kindly way, as was his custom.

"I think a bright young lady such as yourself should always be flattered." The Duke countered with a beaming smile.

"Papa, you will make Rosalind embarrassed." Lady Claudette Blackwood, the Duke's daughter, shook her head a little and laughed.

"I am always being chastised by my daughter." The Duke continued amiably. "What about you, Leighton? Does dear Rosalind here snap at your heels like a hunting dog or boss you around like the fiercest governess?" The Duke clapped a hand on the Earl of Leighton's back.

"Oh, yes. Especially as yuletide draws nearer, it must be said." Rosalind's father laughed and nodded.

"And why do you find yourself more harshly treated at Yuletide?" The Duke was warming to his theme and enjoying it immensely.

Rosalind was enjoying herself very much also. She liked the warm atmosphere at Newfield Hall and had lately found that she had a good deal in common with Claudette, the Duke's daughter. She felt sure that their friendship would continue to grow and that she would, undoubtedly, become a more regular visitor to Newfield Hall on account of it.

"Because that is when Rosalind begins making all her plans for the Christmas celebrations at Leighton Hall. It all seems to begin in November, and so I do what I can to keep out of the way." He laughed.

"Papa!"

"But I must admit, it is always worth it. Rosalind always makes Christmas at Leighton Hall very special indeed. She always finds something a little bit different for us all to do."

"Indeed, she does, I remember well last year's theatrical. Very good, very clever." The Duke turned to Rosalind and smiled.

"Thank you, Your Grace," Rosalind said graciously. "And I must admit, I enjoy it more than anything."

"You do not find so many preparations tiring, Rosalind?" Claudette was studying Rosalind intently. "I mean, it does seem like an awful lot of hard work to lay on a Christmas that is so very full of things to do?"

"It is rather a lot of hard work, but it is something that always excites me. I find that come October I am already thinking of Christmas. It is a most wonderful celebration for everybody, is it not? It is a time for friends and family, and a time to show the staff how much you appreciate their efforts throughout the year. Not to mention a little charity along the way. It is a most charitable time, is it not?"

"Yes, it is. But to manage it all, one must be so very organized," Claudette said with a comical grimace.

"I suppose so, but the skills of organization can very quickly be learned."

"Well, that is settled then," The Duke said, and everybody turned to look at him quizzically.

"What is settled, Papa?" Claudette asked dubiously.

"Claudette, you must arrange Christmas here at Newfield Hall. You must make it exciting and packed with wonderful things to do, just as Rosalind does at Leighton Hall. What do you say?" He had sidled around to his daughter who looked as if she were making ready to run.

"But, Papa."

"My dear girl, you need not look as if you had been cornered in the whole thing."

"But I have, Papa. You have cornered me completely." Claudette laughed, but Rosalind could sense the consternation beneath it all.

"But it would be fun, would it not? It would certainly keep you occupied from now until twelfth night." He shrugged as if he truly were doing her a great favor.

"Well, what sort of things would you like me to arrange, Papa?" Claudette's pretty face was wrinkled in a frown.

"That would be up to you, my dear. You are to have a free hand in all of it. There, am I not a generous father?"

"I do not know how to answer that, Papa, really I do not," Claudette said, and the entire party laughed.

"You never know, Claudette, you might come to enjoy it. I know that it keeps our dear Rosalind happily occupied." Rosalind's mother, Lady Beatrice, was clearly trying to soothe the young woman's nerves.

"Lady Beatrice, I am not as organized as Rosalind." Claudette turned to look at Rosalind for confirmation.

"Claudette, you must not worry about it," Rosalind said gently. "And I will help you, I promise."

"You really will help me?" Claudette looked like a drowning woman who had been thrown a rope.

"Of course, I shall. I shall help you with every bit of it."

"Dear me, what does Claudette need help with?" Suddenly, Gabriel Blackwood, the Duke's son, appeared at Rosalind's side.

He appeared so suddenly that she almost gasped, but hurriedly steadied herself and turned a little to look up at him. Gabriel was very tall, taller even than his father, and standing next to him made Rosalind feel like a child.

"With the Christmas festivities, Gabriel." It was

clear that Claudette had gathered herself a good deal following Rosalind's offer of assistance.

"Oh dear, are we to have Christmas festivities?" Gabriel's tone was flat and, Rosalind thought, just a little sarcastic for her taste.

"Of course, we are, Gabriel. You have not been gone so long that you forget that we celebrate Christmas, have you?" His father laughed but Rosalind thought she detected a little annoyance in his tone.

"Yes, I remember, Father. But I must admit, I remember it being something of a quiet affair." Although his tone was still flat, the sarcasm had very wisely been dispensed with.

"Well, it is time to change all that," The Duke said, also regaining his former jollity.

Rosalind wondered at the cause of the little tension between the two men, and she wondered if anybody else had noticed it. Gabriel had not seemed to enjoy the winter ball his father had thrown at all, and had spent all evening keeping himself in quiet conversation here and there about the large ballroom, and very determinedly avoiding the dancing.

"Yes, we are going to have a much jollier Christmas this year, brother," Claudette said with a bright smile. "And I am going to arrange it. Well, with Rosalind's help, at any rate."

Grab this amazing box set on Kindle Unlimited and read to your hearts delight Christmas Brides and Sweet Kisses

40 Sweet Inspirational Romances

2 book

Special
Edition

Regency romantic dreams – 4 novel-length books

To find all of her books, Follow Charlotte on Amazon Just click the yellow follow button when you get to Amazon.

I hope you enjoyed these books by Charlotte Darcy.

Charlotte is a hopeless romantic. She loves historical romance and the Regency era the most. She has been a writer for many years and can think of nothing better than seeing how her characters can find their happy ever after.

She lives in Derbyshire, England and when not writing you will find her walking the British countryside with her dog Poppy or visiting stately homes, such as Chatsworth House which is local to her.

You can contact Charlotte at CharlotteDarcy@cd2.com or via Facebook at @CharlotteDarcyAuthor

Or join my exclusive newsletter for a free book and updates on new releases here.

The End.

Printed in Great Britain
by Amazon